TWO HEAR⌐ UNSPOKEN PRAYERS

A Christian Romance Story

Nikki Smith

Two Heart's Unspoken Prayers

Two Heart's Unspoken Prayers

DEDICATION

I would like to thank first and foremost, GOD, for giving me the inspiration and drive to write this work. Next, I would like to thank all my family, friends, and fans for their support. Without you guys, I am nothing.

THOUGHTS OF MY LIFE

Who but God can cause a total three-sixty-degree turnaround to occur in a lowly sinner's life? The prophecy was said, the prophecy was written, the prophecy must be done...unless you are somehow blessed to beat it. I'm beating it CHAPTER by Chapter!

Two Heart's Unspoken Prayers

THE STORY

Janine hasn't always lived a life that's on the straight and narrow. Meaning, there was a time in her life when she was a lowly sinner and her relationship with Christ was the very last thing on her mind. But that all changes, and before long, Janine becomes a sista after God's own heart.

But just because she's beautiful, saved, and fabulous, that doesn't mean that all is perfect in paradise. Janine has a college degree, but no matter what she does, she can't seem to snag a decent job with it. She had a fiancée, but he cheated.

When she runs into a single father who's true to his walk with Christ, will God answer both their hearts' unspoken prayers and give them the soulmates they've both been yearning for?

CHAPTER NUMBER ONE

"Girl, you are so lucky, Janine. You have a man who's good-looking, financially stable, saved... *and* he treats you like a princess. Plus, he's not a womanizer like those last two fools you were involved with and dated."

Twenty-six-year-old Janine Grey took a tiny sip from her tall glass of iced tea. Then she gave her best friend, LaVonda, a humble smile. She didn't consider herself to be *lucky* to have Jermaine Rivers in her life. As a woman of faith, she considered herself to be *blessed*.

Janine couldn't help but smile again as she thought about the handsome lawyer who'd strolled into her life a year earlier and brought back her belief that there were some good brothas out there after all.

Grinning, Lavonda continued speaking. "You guys have been dating for almost a year. I bet he's about to pop the question on Valentine's Day next week... You know how romantic he is and all."

At that point, Janine sighed. She'd be lying if she said she hadn't been hoping for and thinking the same thing — hoping that Jermaine was about to ask her to marry him. *Jermaine's a good man,* she thought to herself. *And I've fallen head-over-heels for him. I can easily see the two of us living life together as husband and wife. I can see us starting a family, having a couple of kids together.*

Two Heart's Unspoken Prayers

Janine's eyes met Vonda's across the restaurant table where they were having lunch. "You really think he's about to ask me to marry him, Vonda?"

LaVonda quickly nodded her head. "Yep. I sure do." She grabbed Janine's hand and let out a little giggle. "However, sweetie, you need to make sure you drop by Vanity's and get them to give you the hook-up on your nails before Jermaine gets back into town. That rock — you know the one he might be about to slip on that finger of yours — it's gonna look shabby as sin if your cuticles are looking raggedy."

Grinning, Janine shook her head. Then she pointed at LaVonda's hands. "My nails look just fine, boo. They're neat and well-groomed. I'm just not into all those flashy, high-maintenance manicures like you."

Smiling, LaVonda held her hands up between them and inspected her own fingertips. "Well, you know a girl's gotta pamper herself in some form or fashion. You got that shoe fetish thing that you're into. I've got my fabulous nails." LaVonda giggled. "Are you up to two hundred pairs yet, honey?"

At that point, Janine frowned. "Girl, you know I'm nowhere near that number. I'm barely making ends meet at that dead-end furniture showroom job of mine. It's hard to stay in fabulous footwear on a tight budget—," she set her lips into a thin line then added, "—that is if a sista wanna keep her lights on."

LaVonda pursed her lips, then nodded her head in agreement. "I know, right? That's why I'm glad manicures don't cost all that much if you know where to go…even the nice ones like I get." She paused for a moment then continued speaking. "You know what Janine…both of us are college-educated. We have degrees. You'd think it would be easier than it's been for us to find good-paying jobs."

Janine couldn't help but agree. She, like LaVonda, had graduated from college with a bachelor's degree a few years earlier. Despite her best efforts to send out plenty of résumés and job hunt, she had yet to find any type of reasonable-paying employment in her field of study.

Janine sighed. "The economy's still in a recession, Vonda. All we can both do is keep pressing at it and keep up our faith."

This time it was Vonda's turn to sigh. "Yeah. I guess you're right."

Janine crumpled up her paper napkin and placed it onto her empty plate. "I guess it's about time for me to cut out of here, so I can clock in at that dead-end job that I probably should be a little more grateful to have." She pursed her full lips together. "Bottom line, having something is better than having nothing at all."

Vonda pulled a magazine out of her purse. She had a sly smile on her face. "Wait a minute. I wanted to show you this before you leave. Since I don't have a man right now, it doesn't apply to me. But I thought you might be able to use it."

Janine looked down at the article's headline. It read: *How to Plan a Romantic Evening When You're Hot, Single, & Celibate*. She glanced back over at her friend with a skeptical look in her eyes. "Seriously, Vonda?"

"Yes, *seriously* girl. Just 'cause you're saved and celibate, it doesn't mean you can't have a little bit of romance in your life." She pointed at the glossy magazine. "I personally think you should try out suggestion number two. It says you should plan a surprise dinner for yourself and your boo…you know, with candlelight, soft music, a pretty tablecloth. If you find yourself having trouble planning everything out, don't hesitate to give me a buzz."

At that point, Janine stood up from her chair. She pushed the magazine over towards LaVonda. LaVonda pushed it back.

LaVonda smiled, while shaking her head at the same time. "Just take the magazine, Janine. You might change your mind."

Janine had known her bestie long enough to know she was about to become stubborn about her taking the mag. She gave Vonda a slow little smile. "Um, okay, girl…you win. I'll take it home and take a look at it. That's all I can promise."

*****

Two Heart's Unspoken Prayers

Two Days Later:

Janine's boyfriend, Jermaine, made his way back to his Los Angeles hotel room. He frowned as he glanced down at his cell phone and saw that he had missed two calls, both of them from Janine.

"At least it wasn't my mother calling again, talking that bull about me getting married and giving her some grandkids," he muttered under his breath as he stepped into the elevator that quickly whisked him up to the twenty-third floor.

Seconds later, he walked into the corporate suite that his law firm had rented for him to use during his out-of-state law conference.

He pulled off his designer suit jacket and lowered his lean, muscular body onto the high-end sofa. Then he smiled. Everything was working out just as he knew it would. *Having a girlfriend in my life certainly comes with advantages. Ever since I hooked up with Janine, my mom has at least cut back on some of her nagging about me needing to find a good woman and settle down.*

When his cell phone began buzzing again, he pulled his eyebrows together in a frown. A quick look at the device let him know that it was Janine calling for a third time. Deciding that he'd call her back much later, he swiped the 'missed-call' icon off of the face of his phone and checked his email instead. He couldn't stop the grin that lit up his pecan-tan complexion when he read the email from his boss. He read the message again to make sure that he'd read it right the first time.

"Yeah...that's what I'm talking about! I'm in the running to make partner at Johnson & McMurty!"

He'd barely had time to go over the email message a third time when his phone began ringing yet again. This time he answered it.

The voice of Henry Averson, one of the senior partners at Johnson & McMurty, came over the connection. "Well, Jermaine. I see you just opened my email. I told you I'd be able to convince the old cooter to consider you for partner. Our beloved boss has narrowed it down to two people...you and Patrick Falconi."

Henry paused for a moment, then continued speaking. "Now I'm gonna keep it real with you, man. For some Godforsaken reason, McMurty is a certified barracuda when it comes to law and business, but he has old-fashioned values. He's looking for someone who's not only a kick-butt attorney, but also has a stable family life to take this position." Henry sighed. "I'm sorry to say this, but Patrick Falconi — with his two point five kids and lovely wife — has you beat in that area. I got your foot in the door, but I'm sure McMurty is leaning towards giving Falconi the promotion to partner."

Jermaine frowned. "But I'm more qualified than Patrick Falconi for the job," he said into the phone. "I have more experience. I've won more cases." He shook his head. "And you're gay, Henry.

You're the farthest thing from that traditional family-man that you say McMurty is looking for...yet McMurty promoted *you* to partner."

Henry pursed his lips, then shook his head. "I know I'm gay, Jermaine. You know I'm gay. Everybody knows I'm gay. I don't try to hide that fact...unlike some people I know. But what you're forgetting is that my mother and McMurty's wife are friends. It's my connections that got me my position. Unfortunately, you don't have the same '*connection-angle*' going for yourself."

Jermaine grimaced into the phone. "So, what you're telling me is that if I had a wife and a couple of kids — like Patrick Falconi — I'd have a better shot at making partner at the firm?"

"Yeah, man. That sounds about right." He let out a sarcastic little bark of laughter. "But both of us know that that 'wife-and-kids' thing ain't about to happen." He paused for a moment, then said, "Anyways, I'll see what else I can do to help you out. But on another note, will I be seeing you day after tomorrow when you make it back into town? Pick you up from the airport maybe?"

The wheels in his brain were too busy turning for Jermaine to pay too much attention to Henry's last comment.

"Hello? Earth to Jermaine...did you hear me?"

Bringing his focus back to the phone conversation he was participating in, Jermaine nodded his head. "Yeah, Henry. My flight touches down at eleven-fifteen Monday morning. You picking me up at eleven-forty will be just fine."

The two talked for a few minutes more. Then, trying his best to not make it seem like he was rushing Henry off the phone, Jermaine wrapped up the call.

Jermaine sat there on the sofa for several minutes more. Then a slow smile made its way across his handsome face.

He picked up his cellphone and dialed Janine's number. "I know exactly what to do to solve my little problem," he said under his breath.

*****

Janine quickly wrapped her fluffy towel around her curvy body, which was still damp from her shower. She rushed into her bedroom, hoping to catch her cell phone before it stopped buzzing.

Maybe it's Jermaine calling me back, she thought to herself as she snatched the device up from where it lay on her dresser. "Hello," she said into the phone, while trying not to sound like she was out of breath from the quick sprint from her bathroom.

"Hey, yourself sweetheart. Sorry I missed your calls earlier today. I had my phone turned off...you know, so I wouldn't be distracted during the conference."

Janine grinned. "That's alright, Jermaine. I understand. You didn't become one of Atlanta's most successful up-and-coming attorneys by not taking your job seriously. You're calling me back now. That's what's important."

Yep, I know this little plan is going to work, Jermaine thought to himself after hearing Janine's words. Then he said into the phone, "Thank you for being so understanding, babe. The fact that you're the most gorgeous woman I've ever laid eyes on, and the fact that you're so understanding about my drive to make it in this world—," he intentionally paused for a few seconds for emphasis then continued with, "—those are the two reasons I love you so much."

Janine felt her eyes widen in shock and surprise. Then she switched her cellphone to her other ear. "What did you just say, Jermaine?"

"You're a very special part of my life, Janine. You're a gorgeous, vibrant, wonderful woman. I'm pretty much sure I've fallen in love."

Janine felt her heart go pitter-patter in her chest. What red-blooded sista wouldn't want to hear a man like Jermaine say he had fallen for her. "In love you say?" she whispered into the phone, wearing a tiny smile on her face.

"Yeah, sweetheart…I'm in love with you. Now, I didn't mean to break the news while we're thousands of miles apart. But that's how I feel in my heart. I just couldn't keep it to myself anymore."

Janine was so much in awe from Jermaine's words that she was speechless for several seconds.

Two Heart's Unspoken Prayers

Jermaine felt a slight moment of panic from her lack of a response. But the lawyer in him dictated that he keep his cool. "You still there, sweetheart?"

Janine felt a bit foolish as she nodded her head several times, seeing that she knew he couldn't see her since they were having a phone conversation. Then grinning, she took a deep breath and hurriedly said, "I'm still here, Jermaine."

Jermaine smiled. "Good, baby. Well, I'm not gonna push you to tell me how you feel about me right now. I just needed you to know how I feel about you. I had to get it off my chest. Now, listen...I have to go real quick. The next conference starts in twenty minutes. I don't wanna be late. We'll talk later on this evening, and I can't wait until my flight touches down in Atlanta in two days so I can finally see your gorgeous face again."

As soon as they disconnected their call, Janine closed her eyes and laid her head back into the comfy cushions of her chaise lounge. She let Jermaine's words marinate in her brain for several seconds. "He said that he's fallen in love with me, Lord. He said he's fallen in love."

She opened her eyes again. A smile touched her lips when she happened to catch a glimpse of the magazine that her best friend had given her earlier in the week. She slowly reached over and picked up the glossy mag.

"Hm," she said to her empty living room. "Maybe I'll think about taking Vonda's advice after all.

*****

Four Hours Later:

Vonda brought her treadmill to an abrupt stop at the local gym and gave Janine a big ol' smile. "Girl, I told you so...I told your butt so. I just knew that fine-tail man was falling for you." Vonda couldn't stop grinning. "When's the wedding?"

Janine shook her head and playfully cut her eyes at her bestie. "Girl, he only said he was in love with me and that I was his soulmate. He didn't mention anything about a wedding." She smiled and added, "However, he *did* say something about wanting to see the two of us spending our lives together. And he said he thought we'd make some cute kids together."

At that, Vonda downright squealed. "Girl, he's asking you to marry him as soon as he gets back into town for sure. Probably on Valentine's Day — like I told you the other day." Vonda nodded her head a couple of times. "Yep, you can trust and believe that."

Vonda started the treadmill back up again, but at a much slower pace. Her eyes suddenly lit up in excitement.

Janine groaned. "Oh sweet baby Jesus. I know that look in your eye much too well, LaVonda Robertson."

Vonda somehow managed to paste an innocent expression on her face. "What look, Janine?"

"Uh, you know...the one that means you're about to come up with a crazy idea."

LaVonda's full lips turned up in a tiny smile. "Boo, I'm not trying to come up with some '*crazy idea*'. But I *do* have something in mind."

Janine flashed her bestie a glance filled with doubt. "And what would this '*something*' be?"

Vonda slowed her pace on the treadmill to a crawl. "Well, you have the key to Jermaine's place, compliments of you going over there and feeding that beast of a dog of his ever since he went out of town."

Janine frowned. "Yeah, that's true. But what does that have to do with anything?"

"Well, sweetie...I think you should pull out that magazine I gave you the other day and reread that article on *How to Plan a Romantic Evening when you're Saved, Hot, & Celibate.* Then I think you should go feed that dog of Jermaine's, and while you're at his house, set up a romantic little dinner table in that sunroom of his." Her eyes met Janine's. "He gets back in town Monday evening, right?"

Janine sighed. "Yeah."

"Well, I suggest you take a half-day off Monday, show up at his place around noon — you know, before he gets home — and set everything up." Vonda's eyes lit up. "I'm sure you're aware I love planning little get-togethers and decorating and all. I can help you out and disappear before he walks through the front door."

Janine set her lips in a half-smile/half-frown. Then her eyes slowly brightened. Then she grinned. "You know what Vonda... I actually like that idea."

LaVonda brought her exercise machine to a full stop. "In that case, let's call it quits in here and go plan-out your '*hot, saved, and celibate*' romantic dinner for two."

CHAPTER NUMBER TWO

Janine glanced around Jermaine's tastefully decorated four-season sunroom, then she laid eyes on Vonda and frowned.

"What's wrong now, Janine?" Vonda waved her hand around the room. "You don't like how we set up the makeshift dining table or something? You still think the black lace tablecloth was a bit too much?"

Janine grimaced. "No. It's not that. I actually think you did an A-plus job on everything…from the candlelight to the flowers and the dinnerware. Everything. It's just that….um, don't you think Jermaine will be tired when he gets in from his flight?" She sighed. "This was probably a bad idea."

Vonda cut her eyes at Janine. "Girl, that man said he's in love with your behind. He may be tired, but he's gonna be thrilled when he gets home this evening."

Still worried, Janine said, "But what if his flight is delayed or something?"

Vonda shook her head, then smiled. "Stop worrying, Janine. The weather's pretty stable across the whole country. Plus, he's on a non-stop flight from L.A. to here. If you had gotten his flight number — like I told you to do — we could look everything up. But in the meantime, boo…stop worrying. He'll be here at seven this evening and he'll be happy to see you."

With that said, Vonda glanced down at her wristwatch. "Since it's close to noon, that only gives us about two hours to get to the grocery store and pick up everything we need to prepare your surprise welcome-home dinner. Plus, we gotta get you that manicure and get your hair slayed. Get your coat, sweetie. Let's get ready to go."

Right after the words came out of Vonda's mouth, both Vonda and Janine looked at each other with shocked eyes as the house security alarm began to go off.

Janine's heart stopped jumping in her chest when she heard Jermaine's voice and realized that it wasn't an intruder. Then a feeling that was a mixture of shock and disbelief settled into her soul when the alarm was quickly deactivated and a second masculine voice said, "Let me get the zipper on those slacks, Jermaine, baby....so you can work what your daddy gave you. The video-phone sex we had the past few days wasn't enough for me. I've been waiting for you to rock my world all week."

Janine saw red. It didn't take the sexual sounds that were now coming from Jermaine's living room for her to figure out what was going on. "That snake," she hissed under her breath as she broke out into a run towards the front of the house.

With his pants and designer underwear in a pool around his ankles, Jermaine looked up at Janine. His eyes were as big as twin brown saucers.

Two Heart's Unspoken Prayers

Janine was normally a mild-mannered person. But the compromising position in which she saw the man who'd just confessed to loving her so much only days earlier, took her over the top.

"You lying, no-good, MF'er! What happened to all your sweet words of being in love with me, Jermaine?!"

Because of the flaming wrath in Janine's eyes, Henry Averson — who was Jermaine's co-worker and a senior law partner at Johnson & McMurty — stepped back from his lover.

Janine paid the buff, blonde-haired man no attention...she didn't have a problem with him. "Like I said, Jermaine...what gives, bruh?! You called me on the phone from Los Angeles with all your confessions of undying love! Talking about us having kids! Us having a life together!"

Jermaine's face was emotionless when he said, "You weren't supposed to be here, Janine."

"Wasn't supposed to be here?! Wasn't supposed to freaking be here?!"

Vonda had known Janine long enough to realize that despite her normally reserved character, right now, her best friend was ready to draw blood.

Vonda grabbed Janine by the arm. "He's not worth it, boo. His trifling behind's an attorney. He'll probably find some way to sue the both of us if we put our feet up his black behind like he deserves."

Vonda shook her head. Then her eyes shot daggers at Jermaine. "You're a real piece of work,

Jermaine. A real piece of work. Get yo purse, Janine…let's go."

*****

Later that Night:

Janine sat alone in her apartment, dabbing at the tears in the corners of her eyes. She felt so betrayed. After a long line of failed relationships, she really had believed God had answered her prayers and blessed her with a good man. She'd felt it was a miracle that Jermaine had been willing to date her for a year despite the fact that she'd told him from the get-go that she was celibate.

She shook her head and closed her eyes. "Lord, now I understand why. He was getting his rocks off with no-telling how many people on the side... Probably men and women both."

She laid her head back into the sofa cushions and began reflecting on her life. "I'm tired of everything, Lord. My job, my love-life, this city. I need a change."

CHAPTER NUMBER THREE

A Month Later:

"Well, what are you gonna do, Janine?"

Janine looked at her best friend, LaVonda. She shook her head and said, "I don't know."

LaVonda reached into the front pocket of her designer jeans and pulled out a penny. She grabbed Janine's hand and pressed the shiny, brown coin against her girl's palm. "Well, in that case then — since you're not sure what to do about it and all — here's a penny for *my* thoughts. In other words, I'm gonna tell you what I think you should do about it." A broad smile stretched LaVonda's face when she excitedly said, "I think you should take the job."

Janine frowned. "Take it? But it's way up in North Carolina...two states away from here. Two states away from my friends and family."

Still smiling, LaVonda cut her eyes at Janine. "Yep, Durham may be two states away, but it's only a six-hour drive away from us here in Atlanta. That's a whole lot closer than the Big Apple. You know durn well me, you, and Sharon used to drive up there all the time just to party or catch some big-name concert."

Janine grimaced. Since turning her life over to the Lord, driving five states away at the drop of a hat for a good time had become a thing of the past.

23

Yeah, she still liked to have fun like the next sista, but not to such extremes. She shook her head. "I don't know, Vonda."

LaVonda squinched her almond-shaped eyes together and began wagging her finger in the air. "Janine Denise Grey...this is a once-in-a-lifetime offer. You *have* to take it. You've been praying for a job opportunity like this ever since we graduated from Savannah State three years ago."

Janine sighed, as she thought about her close to minimum wage job selling furniture in a big-box store's showroom. "I know I've been praying for a job like this...but I'm gonna miss you guys."

Seated side-by-side on Janine's overstuffed sofa, LaVonda couldn't help but lean in towards Janine's shoulder and give her a warm, heartfelt hug. "You know all of us here in the ATL are gonna miss your behind, too — especially me. You've only been my bestie since kindergarten. But like I said, opportunities like this only come once-in-a-lifetime."

Janine knew her girl was right. In fact, LaVonda was saying the exact same thing both her parents had told her the night before. She knew she should take the job.

She gave Vonda a smile that was both happy and sad at the same time. Then she said, "Well, I guess I'm about to become a card-carrying member of the American Airlines' frequent-flyer club."

Vonda grinned. "Me too. After all, flying from here to Durham only takes about an hour-and-

24

a-half." She winked her eye. "And you know I already checked."

Vonda was well known amongst their little circle of friends for being an information hound…some people even called her nosy. But Janine couldn't help but love her girl because Vonda had a good heart.

At that point Janine let a tiny chuckle escape from her lips. "Sweetie, thanks for looking into that. An hour-and-a-half long flight ain't bad at all." She shook her head for emphasis. "Nope, it ain't bad at all."

LaVonda gave Janine another quick hug then stood up from the sofa. She grinned. "Good. Now that we got that all settled and you're taking the job, I can cut outta here and make it to Jordan's right before they close. I've been having a hankering for their chocolate turtle cheesecake all week. Plus, who knows…maybe you'll find your Mr. Right while you're up there. I read somewhere — I think it was Essence — that North Carolina has a healthy dose of eligible bachelors." LaVonda chuckled. "Shoot girl, based on how limited the dating pool is down here in the ATL right now, a sista is starting to think she might have to find her a job up there in North Carolina and join you. I'm tired of dating duds and being single."

Smiling, Janine shook her head. "You're a mess, LaVonda. I'm not going up there to find a man, I'm going for the job."

Two Heart's Unspoken Prayers

Seconds after her front door had closed behind her bestie, Janine flopped back down on her sofa and sighed. "Well Lord, I asked you for a sign on whether or not I should take the job. Then you sent LaVonda over here to tell me to go for it." She nodded her head. "That's confirmation enough for me. I guess I'm moving to North Carolina."

*****

A Month Later:

Janine smoothed her hand down the front of her Armani suit and checked her reflection a final time in the full-length mirror in her apartment. She was happy that the girl at the thrift store had talked her into buying the dark gray pantsuit a week earlier. Yeah, she'd had to shell out a hundred bucks on the garment, then get a tailor to take the waist in. But the used suit — which she was sure had cost someone around a thousand dollars new — looked good on her curvy body and boosted her confidence for her first day at her new job.

It only took her about twenty minutes to complete her commute to work. As soon as she pulled into the spacious parking lot, Janine claimed an empty spot outside of the modern-looking, three-story brick building that housed Blackstone Manufacturing. She stepped out into the cool spring morning air and made her way through the glass-paned, double doors of her new workplace.

"Good morning, how can I help you?"

Two Heart's Unspoken Prayers

Janine directed a friendly smile at the receptionist at the desk towards the side of the lobby. "Good morning, I'm Janine Grey. I'm a new employee."

Grinning, the woman quickly nodded her head. "Yes, yes. You're the new hire for Mr. Blackstone's design assistant position." She extended her palm for a handshake. "I'm Denise...Denise Madison. I was on maternity leave when you came for your interview last month. Otherwise, we would've met already."

Janine could tell right away that she liked Denise.

The tall, brown-skinned girl continued speaking. "Did they give you a tour of the building when you came in for your interview last month?"

Janine nodded her head. "Kinda sorta. Mr. Cherry interviewed me and then he gave me a quick walk-through of the place. He said he was sorry to rush, but he had a tight deadline. Something about a project he was working on."

"Yeah. That would've been the spring furniture market showing that he was talking about. Since the business owner — Mr. Blackstone — was out of town on some family business for the past couple of months, a lot of the work around here fell into Mr. Cherry's lap." Denise frowned, but only for a moment. "But any-hootie, do you remember how to get to your office? It's on the second floor. Once you step out the elevator, you hang a right and go all the way to the end of the hallway."

Janine grinned again. "Yes. I remember the office that Mr. Cherry showed me."

At that moment, the phone on Denise's desk began to buzz. Janine gave the girl a friendly wave goodbye as she made her way to the elevator in the center of the lobby.

Seconds later, after the elevator swooshed to a stop, she took a deep breath and stepped out into the brightly lit, empty hallway.

"Lord," she uttered in a low voice as a million butterflies flitted in her stomach, "if it be within your will, let my first day here go by without a hitch."

As soon as the words came out of her mouth, Janine frowned at the pair of deep masculine voices that she heard coming from the open office door at the very end of the hallway. She'd only talked to Mr. Cherry a couple of times — once on the telephone, the second time during her interview and tour — but Janine was pretty much sure that one of the voices belonged to him. The other voice, she'd never heard before, but she was concerned about the words that the unknown man had just spoken...not that she'd meant to eavesdrop on their conversation, of course.

As bright sunlight filtered into the spacious office of the CEO of Blackstone Manufacturing, Donovan Cherry frowned at his boss. "Trust me on this, Nate...Janine Grey is a perfect fit for the position. You've been saying for almost a year now that we need to bring a fresh, young perspective into the pieces that we put out on the market. Janine Grey's design portfolio was phenomenal. I'm sure she's the one for the job."

Nate Blackstone leaned back in his leather office recliner and tented his fingers. His eyes met those of his company's vice president and friend, Donovan. He sighed.

Donovan continued speaking. "I know you haven't had a chance to take a look at her designs, seeing that you've been out of town for the last month and a half...but trust me on this one, Nate. This girl is something special. I offered her a contract right away. I didn't wanna let her fall through the cracks."

Nate stood up from his chair. "Well, I hope you're right, Donnie. She's been out of college for three long years, and she's only been working on a furniture sales floor during that whole time. If she's as good as you say she is, I'm sure she's been sending résumés out to different furniture manufacturing companies." He sighed. "But nobody's been willing to take her on. That makes me believe that there might be some type of problem with her."

At that, Donovan frowned. "Come on Nate, you for one should know how hard it is for a person of color to break into the furniture business. Trust me man, Janine Grey has some real talent."

Janine had never met the CEO and owner of Blackstone Manufacturing, but hearing the way he was talking about her made her blood boil. She shook her head as she turned on her heel and made her way down the opposite end of the hallway towards her tiny office.

Seeing that it was her first day on the job, she hadn't wanted anything to go wrong. Consequently, she'd made sure to arrive thirty minutes or so early. Since the half-dozen or so offices that she'd passed along the way to her own space seemed to be empty, she figured she must have beat the majority of the other employees into work that morning.

The nerve of the man, she thought to herself as she took a seat behind her office desk. *He hasn't even looked at my designs and he's already passing judgement…insinuating that I must not be any good at designing because I haven't been able to snag a freaking job!*

For a moment, she felt like marching down the hallway to his office and telling Nate Blackstone to his face that he could just take his job and shove it where the sun didn't shine. But then common sense kicked in. In her heart of hearts, she knew that would be the wrong move.

"It took a good chunk of my meager savings relocating from Atlanta to here," she muttered under her breath to herself. "I need this job….it pays three times what I made selling furniture in the Rooms to Go showroom. Plus, it's given me the change of environment I've been praying for."

She shook her head. "Lord, I don't like this Nate Blackstone, but I'll be durned if I'm gonna let him ruin this opportunity for me. I'm fighting to keep this job."

"Ms. Grey, I see you made it in early."

Janine had been so caught up in her thoughts that she hadn't noticed Donovan Cherry peeking his head into her open office doorway.

Donovan smiled. "Oh, I didn't scare you, did I? If I did, I'm sorry. I wasn't expecting you to be in the office yet. Your workday doesn't officially start 'til nine."

Janine actually liked Donovan Cherry. He seemed to be a nice guy. She gave him a genuine smile. "Good morning, Mr. Cherry. I thought I'd come in early and get a feel for the place...seeing that it's my first day."

Donovan nodded his head in approval. "Good. You're a go-getter. I like that. The rest of the crew should be coming in any minute now." He smiled. "I'll go ahead and get out of your hair and let you get settled into your office. Then at around nine-fifteen, you can come downstairs to the design floor, and I'll introduce you to everybody. That okay with you?"

Janine flashed him another smile. "Of course."

*****

An hour later, with the exception of Nate Blackstone — who she had yet to meet — Janine was sure she was going to like working with all the other employees at her new job.

Angela Layton, Blackstone's quality control specialist, gave Janine a smile then said, "It's good to have another individual of the feminine persuasion joining the Blackstone team. There's only a handful of us ladies here. But that's really not uncommon in the furniture manufacturing business. I know this is your first day and you've only just met us, but do you think you're gonna like working here, Janine?"

Janine pushed all thoughts of the conversation she'd inadvertently heard that morning between Nate Blackstone and Donovan Cherry to the back of her mind. So far, the business owner himself seemed to be the only gray cloud on her horizon.

She returned Angela's smile then nodded her head. "Yep, I think I'm gonna like it here just fine."

"Good. Now Donovan told me a few days ago that you just relocated here to Durham from Atlanta. Have you had a chance to get out and explore the city?"

"No. Not really."

"Well, in that case, if you're interested, me and Denise — you know, she's the receptionist downstairs — we would be happy to take you on a quick tour of the place we call home. We could do it one day this week. And we're having Bible study this Wednesday evening at our church. You're more than welcome to come out and join us."

Finding a new church home had been at the top of Janine's to-do-list. She shared as much with Angela.

Angela grinned. "Well, in that case then Janine, if you like having a Holy Ghost, foot-stomping, God-praising, soul-saving good time, you're gonna love Faith Tabernacle. You can trust and believe me on that."

A smile worked its way onto Janine's lips. From Angela's enthusiastic description, she was sure that she could believe her about having a good time at her church. *Ain't nothing wrong with getting worked up for the Lord,* she thought to herself.

*****

Later that Afternoon:

After spending the morning and most of the afternoon updating himself on Blackstone Manufacturing's latest accounts, Nate finally reached into his desk and pulled out Janine Grey's portfolio and résumé. As he studied the pieces of furniture that she'd designed, he couldn't help but admit that his friend and vice-president, Donovan, had been right. The woman had a type of raw talent that he hadn't really ever seen before.

As he finished marveling over the last design in her portfolio, he reached over and slowly opened her résumé. Right below her name was a small photo of a woman that he assumed was Janine Grey. For some reason, he couldn't seem to pull his eyes away from the image. The girl in the photograph was beautiful. But it was something about the look in her eyes that seemed to hold him transfixed.

After staring at the picture for close to half a minute, Nate frowned. He shook his head, then quickly skimmed through the rest of her résumé. When he got to the last page, he read the personal statement that she'd closed her résumé with. Then he read it for a second time. Being brutally honest, Janine Grey had admitted that she lacked experience in the furniture world, but that she was a believer in hard work and making sure she became an asset to whatever company she worked for.

After he'd finally closed the very professional-looking folder that she'd chosen to present herself to his company in, Nate leaned back into the soft leather of his office chair and tented his fingers together deep in thought. Something in his soul was telling him that there was something special about Janine Grey. For some odd reason, that both shocked and disturbed him, while intriguing him at the same time. He frowned.

CHAPTER NUMBER FOUR

Janine had been at Blackstone Manufacturing for nine days and had yet to meet the business owner and CEO, Nate Blackstone. She was beginning to think that by some miracle, she'd never have to deal face-to-face with the man.

Needless to say, her dreams of not meeting her boss were quickly dashed when Nate Blackstone himself shot her an email requesting that she meet him in his office at ten-thirty the following morning.

Angela looked across the drafting table at Janine. Angela was wearing a frown on her pretty light brown face. "You're normally smiling and cheerful… What's wrong?"

Janine grimaced. "I told you the other day that I hadn't met our boss yet, but all of that is about to change. He wants to speak to me in his office tomorrow morning."

Angela shook her head. "I don't understand why you don't wanna meet him, Janine. Nate Blackstone is a nice guy. A really nice guy."

With thoughts of the conversation that she'd overheard between Nate Blackstone and Donovan Cherry fresh on her mind, Janine grimaced. She hadn't known Angela for very long, but she considered her to be a friend.

Two Heart's Unspoken Prayers

Since they were alone in the drafting room, Janine quickly filled Angela in on what had happened her first day at work. In other words, she told Angela what Nate Blackstone had said about her and how he doubted her abilities to perform her job.

Angela heard Janine out then said, "Now I'm not taking sides on this or anything mind you, but I think you could maybe look at the situation from a slightly different angle. You said Nate — uh, I mean Mr. Blackstone — had never seen your work before...right?"

Janine nodded her head yes.

Angela smiled then continued speaking. "Well, that right there is half of the problem. You've been here for almost two weeks, and I can tell that you're a very talented furniture designer. You have some serious skills, girlfriend."

Janine felt the heat of a blush warm her cheeks from Angela's compliment. She thanked the other girl for her kind words.

Angela set her pencil down on the long table. "Now that we both understand you're good at what you do, you need to look at it like this—". Her eyes met Janine's. "The boss hadn't seen your work when he made his comment. Therefore, it's just a simple matter of him seeing what you can do. Once that happens, all this worry you have and dislike for him is gonna be over with. He's one of the good guys. Trust me, I've met enough buttholes in my thirty years to know."

Two Heart's Unspoken Prayers

Despite her knowing that everything Angela had said made sense, Janine still couldn't fully get past how casually Nate Blackstone had dismissed her.

"In his email, did he at least mention what he wants to talk to you about?" Angela asked.

Janine shook her head. "Nope."

"Well, you never know, honey—," Angela smiled, "—he could be wanting to congratulate you on what a good job you've been doing around here."

For some reason, Janine highly doubted it. But, since Angela seemed to be such a Nate Blackstone fan, she decided to keep her final thoughts on the subject to herself and move the conversation over to a different topic.

"You know, Angela, I've been giving that invite you gave me to the singles meet-and-greet conference at Faith Tabernacle some serious thought. It sounds good, but I think I'm gonna sit it out."

Angela crinkled her eyebrows together in a frown. "Sit it out? Honey, I thought you said you were tired of being single. This event only happens once a year. All the eligible, saved men in the city and surrounding areas are gonna be all up in there."

Now it was Janine's turn to grimace. "I'm just tired of going to events like that. Some people get lucky — or I guess you can say blessed. But they never pan out for me."

"Alright. I feel you."

*****

The Following Morning:

Janine hated to admit that the extra effort that she was putting into her outfit that day had a lot to do with having to meet up with her boss. She loved her new job and based on what she'd heard Nate Blackstone say about her, she knew she already had a mark against her. She didn't want to give him any reason — even her clothing — to think even less of her than what he already did.

She arrived at Blackstone Manufacturing at her usual time and spent a little over an hour working on a drafting project. The time on the clock ticked closer and closer to 10:30 — the time she was supposed to be meeting with Nate Blackstone. So, she stood up from the drafting table and began making her way upstairs to his office.

She waved at the receptionist on the executive floor then began walking down the hallway. When she made it to his office, she was expecting the door to be closed. It wasn't. She was expecting him to be inside, but that wasn't the case either. However, there was a little girl in there, one who couldn't have been more than four years old. The child was sitting quietly as she doodled on a sketchpad using a purple crayon.

Janine stepped into the office and smiled at the little girl. Then she said, "Hello." But the child didn't say anything in return. She didn't even smile.

In fact, she acted as if Janine wasn't even there at all.

Maybe she's deaf. That's what Janine thought to herself as she proceeded to try to wave hello instead. Still no luck.

Janine really did love kids, so, even though she didn't know who the cute little girl belonged to, she still wanted to try to communicate with her.

Janine had brought a writing pad and an ink pen with her to the office — just in case she needed to take notes. She pulled the ink pen off the notepad and quickly sketched an image of a hand waving hello. She smiled and held the image up so the little girl could see it. Then she said, "hello," again. This time, Janine was rewarded with a smile, and that pleased her.

Good. We're making progress.

"My name is Ms. Janine. What's your name?"

Janine waited about five seconds, but she got no response again, so, she pointed at her own chest a couple of times using her index finger. She smiled and said, "Ms. Janine." Then she pointed at the little girl and asked, "And you are?"

The little girl began writing on the sketch pad in her lap. Janine stepped closer so that she could see what she was writing. The child had written a single word. The word was Lisa.

Janine smiled. "Ok. It's nice to meet you, Lisa."

Two Heart's Unspoken Prayers

There was a chair located in front of the desk, right beside the one that the little girl was sitting on. Janine sat down on the empty chair. Then she pulled out a long piece of string that she just so happened to have in her pocket. She tied the ends of the string so that the string formed a giant O. She hadn't done it in a long time, but she began making figures with the piece of string using her fingers. First, she made a box shape. Then she made a more intricate shape that was made of several triangles. Her antics made the child smile, and the little girl even reached out and touched the string a couple of times.

They played together with the string for several minutes, then Janine figured it was time for a change of pace — she didn't want the child to get bored.

Being an architect, Janine had excellent drawing skills. So, she quickly sketched a picture of an apple. She drew a picture of a heart shape right next to it. She smiled again and said "I love apples. What about you?"

The little girl's eyes began to sparkle, and she nodded her head and smiled.

Janine chuckled. "Excellent."

Janine stayed there communicating with the child in that manner for a good two or three minutes. Then she heard a deep, masculine voice behind her say, "Sorry I'm late, Ms. Grey. I had to take an emergency call from a client. But all's fine now, and—"

Two Heart's Unspoken Prayers

Nate stopped speaking mid-sentence when he noticed his daughter pull on the sleeve that belonged to the woman that he was talking to. He furrowed his brow when his beautiful, autistic, normally non-verbal child whispered, "Ms. Janine like apple."

She's talking. My baby's talking. She's saying words outside of the normal four that she usually only says. In his heart, he was convinced he was witnessing a miracle.

Nate fixed a grin on his face that was brighter than the sun. He couldn't help but pick up his little girl and give her a hug. As he held her close to his heart, he said, "And you like apples, too... Right, pumpkin?"

The little girl didn't say a word. She simply nodded her head.

Watching the interaction playing out in front of her, Janine knew something was wrong...no, she knew something was very right. And whatever that something was, she knew it was extraordinary. She didn't know Nate Blackstone — had never even spoken to the man before in her life — but the look on his face, the look in his eyes was saying volumes.

Nate wanted to stay there holding his child forever, but he knew they had to get on with their day. Whatever miracle God had in the works, he was glad for it. Grinning, he finally pulled back from his daughter and said, "Are you ready to go downstairs to the daycare center, Pumpkin?"

Once again, Lisa didn't respond. That made Nate sad, but his heart was still rejoicing. He'd seen the first signs of progress in his daughter that day. He turned his attention to Janine. "If you can give me a second, Ms. Grey, I need to take my daughter downstairs to the daycare real quick."

Janine nodded. "Of course." She smiled at Lisa. She winked an eye. "See you later, Lisa. I hope you get an apple today."

The little girl giggled. "Apple!"

To Janine's surprise, her father laughed, too.

As soon as he stepped out of the office, Janine scrunched her face up, confused. She couldn't figure out for the life of her what she'd just witnessed. If she knew Nate Blackstone, she was certain that she would've questioned him once he returned to his office. But since she didn't know him from Adam, she was leaving it alone.

She frowned. *He already doesn't think I'm qualified for this job — he probably doesn't even like me.*

Five minutes later, she was receiving the shock of the hour.

"Uh, excuse me, Mr. Blackstone," she said as she sat across from him at his desk as he smiled at her. "Can you repeat that please?"

Nate placed Janine's employee profile folder back down on his desk. "I said that I looked over your résumé, and I think you're gonna be an asset to Blackstone Manufacturing."

Two Heart's Unspoken Prayers

She had thought that's what he had said the first time, but after she'd overheard him and Donovan talking about her, she couldn't believe her ears.

He smiled. "You look surprised to hear me say that. I understand that you haven't worked hands-on in the industry before now, but the design examples that you included with your résumé impressed me."

Now it was her turn to smile. Not only did she smile, but she also blushed. "Um, thank you, Mr. Blackstone."

"You're welcome. But I'm just stating facts. Now on to the reason that I called this meeting with you in the first place. I have a special line of bedroom furniture that I'm starting for the young adult set. I was hoping to get your input—" He shook his head. "I take that back; I was hoping that we could collaborate on it. You're closer to that age demographic, so I was thinking that you'd be more in touch with what they would want. Know what I mean?"

She nodded. "Of course."

"Good. I'll send you the sketches of the designs that I already have in mind. You can tweak 'em for me and send 'em back. Does a week deadline sound good to you?"

Janine suspected that a week was more than enough. She wasn't arrogant, it was simply her confidence in her skills and the fact that she knew that she knew her stuff. But since she had just

43

started at her new job, she figured that there was nothing wrong with giving herself a little extra leeway on her first major design project. So, she said, "A week will be just fine, Mr. Blackstone."

He grinned again. "Excellent."

Janine had walked into her boss' office that day prepared to dislike him, by the time she walked out, she understood why her coworkers had kept telling her that he was an okay person to work for.

She took the elevator back down to the floor that the company's shared drafting area was located on. She was almost to the space when Angela popped out of the supply closet with a box of colored pencils in hand. "Well, how'd it go, Janine?"

Janine stopped walking and tilted her head to the side as scenes from the meeting she'd just had with her boss danced through her brain. She smiled. "You know, you were right. He's not that bad at all. I think I'mma look forward to working with him. He's sending me some sketches for his new young adult line."

An 'I-told-you-so' look materialized on Angela's face, then she laughed.

Janine smiled. "Okay, like I said, you were right... He's a nice guy. And he complimented me on my designs that I sent with my résumé, too. He said that he looks forward to seeing more of what I can do."

Angela nodded his head then said, "Wow, he wants you to work on his young adult line." She stuck her hand up in the air in front of Janine. "Give me a high-five girl. That's his latest baby. He must really trust you to wanna have you work on that. Congratulations, Janine."

Surprised, Janine couldn't help but cheese. "Thanks."

Janine was whistling a happy tune as she finally sat down at one of the drafting tables. *I guess things aren't gonna be that bad working with him after all.*

*****

At the end of the business day, Nate walked down to the daycare center on the first floor of his building. He was ready to pick up his child.

As soon as he walked in, he threw a smile at Mrs. Reed, the center's supervisor.

"Hey, there, Mr. Blackstone. We're getting Lisa ready to go for you. She'll be ready in a couple of minutes."

After Lisa had been more communicative early that day with Janine, Nate was anxious to hear about what his little angel had said since the time he'd dropped her off that morning. He had been praying on it off and on that day, and being a man of faith, he had confidence that God could show up and show out. "How did she do today?" he asked, expecting a positive report.

Mrs. Reed knew what he was hoping for, and she felt sorry for her employer. Nate always came in the daycare with such high hopes for his daughter. Unfortunately, Lisa wasn't making any progress in interacting with anyone. She was locked in her own world, and she only spoke a handful of words, and those were spoken sporadically — like one or two words every couple of days.

"Well, she drew in her sketchbook with her crayons."

"That was it?"

She hated to dash his hopes, but she had no choice but to tell the truth. "Yep. That's it."

"Okay."

Five minutes later, Nate carefully placed Lisa into her booster seat and strapped her in. He'd made sure that his business had a daycare, because he'd felt it important that his employees not have to worry about childcare. However, due to his daughter having autism, he normally didn't bring her to his facility's daycare center because they didn't offer specialized care. But Nate figured that wouldn't have made a difference anyway. He'd tried specialized one-on-one treatment for Lisa, but it hadn't worked. So, most of the time, his mother babysat her during the day, while he took over at nights.

His mind landed on Lisa's mother — his ex — the woman who'd deserted her own child when she found out that Lisa was special needs. He frowned just from thinking about it. He couldn't imagine life without his daughter. Her smile lit up

his day. He thanked God constantly that He'd
decided to bless him with her.

CHAPTER NUMBER FIVE

Janine loved the fact that she had a private office at work — it sure did come in handy — but she was surprised to realize that she preferred working in the large drafting room that had huge tables that she and her coworkers could share. She figured it was partly because the area was so light and cheery, but mostly because she really liked all the employees at Blackstone Manufacturing. She hadn't met a single coworker that rubbed her the wrong way the entire two weeks she'd worked there.

After the little mishap/misunderstanding with her boss had been cleared up, she had to admit that she even liked him, too. As they'd ended their little talk yesterday, she had realized there was something that she really admired about Nate Blackstone — she just couldn't quite put her finger on it.

One of her favorite scriptures suddenly popped up in her head, Romans 8:28 — *And we know that in all things God works for the good of those who love him, who have been called according to his purpose.* Janine knew for a fact that the scripture was true. Yes, Jermaine cheating on her like he had — violating the trust that she'd had in him — had hurt her badly. But she was certain she never would've taken a job two states away if he hadn't. God had severed her connection with someone who would've ended up hurting her even more if she'd married him, while blessing her at the same time.

Sitting there in the drafting room, she closed her eyes, opened her hands and held them up as if she were receiving a blessing. Then she whispered, "To God be the glory."

She didn't notice Nate walking into the room as she gave God a moment of praise, but it wouldn't have mattered to her anyway. Why? When God put it on Janine's heart to give Him some glory, she'd learned a long time ago to simply obey.

Nate had been on his way to the drafting table to talk to his newest employee about the project he'd assigned her yesterday, but he stopped his forward motion when he noticed she was praying. He considered himself to be a man of faith, so he always gave God his proper respect. Her prayer only lasted about ten seconds, and as soon as she began sketching again, Nate resumed his approach.

"Good morning, Ms. Grey."

The floors were carpeted, so Janine hadn't heard Nate's footfalls when he'd come into the drafting room. Neither had she heard him opening the room's door — its hinges were well-oiled, so it hadn't made a sound.

She jumped in her chair, startled.

"Oh, I didn't mean to scare you," he apologized.

She looked up at her boss and grinned. She shook her head. "No problem, Mr. Blackstone. I was just having a moment of um—"

"Prayer," he interrupted. He winked an eye. "Ain't no shame in that." He waved a hand around himself. "In fact, this workplace encourages it. None of this would be possible without the Lord's intervention." He thumbed his chest a couple of times and said, "Li'l ol' Nate Blackstone didn't have the power to make this corporation happen." He pointed upwards. "But the Lord did."

Janine grinned. She'd finally identified the 'something different' she'd noticed about her boss yesterday. It was Holiness — his salvation — he had it written all over him. She assumed it was her being mad about what he'd said to Donovan that had caused her to fail to initially notice it.

She grinned. "Amen, boss," she replied. She knew she was about to go into an area that didn't have a thing to do with work, but she was gonna do it anyway because she had felt a draw to his daughter — she'd even had a dream about the little girl last night. So, she asked, "How's Lisa?"

Being that she was an autistic individual who was mostly non-verbal, Lisa barely ever talked — not even to her father. But that didn't stop Nate from being a proud parent. He loved his little girl with his all. Accordingly, he smiled and said, "She's doing fine. We have a daycare here in the building — as you probably already know from what happened yesterday — but my mother normally babysits Lisa. My mom is in the Bahamas on vacation for the next four weeks — it's really a cruise of the Caribbean — so I've been having to make do with alternative arrangements…aka, the daycare. Not that there's anything wrong with our daycare facility here in the building, it's just that—"

Janine interrupted him with, "It's just that changes in her schedule upsets and confuses her." She frowned. "Poor baby…bless her sweet little heart."

She gets it. Nate could instantly tell that Janine understood his daughter's plight. He could also tell that not only did she understand, but she also empathized. He could see her feelings written all over her face.

Janine's eyes met his. "Lisa has autism, doesn't she?"

"Yes, how did you know?"

"My little cousin—," she grinned, "—correction, I gotta say my younger cousin, because he's much taller and bigger than me now, seeing that he's only four years younger than myself. Anyhow, he has autism. He was much like your precious little angel when we were younger. There were only three words he used to say to most people…up until he was around seven-years-old."

The fact that she had said '*used to*' really piqued Nate's interest. It made him think that Janine's cousin had advanced past only using a handful of words to communicate. He wanted the same thing for his daughter.

Janine chuckled. "As I said, he only used three words with most people because when he and I talked together, he used many more words with me — and only with me. Eventually, that spilled over into him being more vocal with everyone else." A thoughtful look came on her face. "It was like he would pick up words from me like a sponge, but he didn't use them when he was talking to other people until he was a little older." She nodded her head. "Like I was saying, not until he was around seven-years-old."

"So, you helped him to expand his vocabulary?"

"Yeah, I guess you could say that. None of his therapists could get him to do it — they were stumped, but my grandma always said that I had a magic touch." She smiled. "Well actually, my grandmother said that I had a gift in that way, in that area…that God had blessed me with something within myself that my cousin responded to. Grandma called it a blessing. In fact, back when I was in college, I had considered becoming a speech language pathologist or a therapist because of my experience with my cousin. But in the end, my passion for design won out. Although, I can't say that someday, I'm not gonna go back to college and get a second degree so I can become a therapist."

Based on the way he was looking at her, Janine could tell that something was wrong. *Did I say too much? Is he now gonna start thinking that I'm not really into my job here at Blackstone Manufacturing?*

She tilted her head to the side and asked, "What is it, Mr. Blackstone? Is something the matter?"

Nate drew his eyebrows together. He shook his head. "No, nothing's wrong. I was just thinking about something."

He paused for a few seconds, trying to figure out the best way to say his next words. He finally just sighed and said, "Well, I guess I might as well just go ahead and lay it all out...you know, explain it to you up front."

"Okay."

His eyes met hers. Then he said, "Up until yesterday, my little girl only had four words in her vocabulary: No, yes, eat, and play. Those were the only four words she's said for the past two years. When Lisa and I got home last night, she had two new words." He smiled. "Well, three if you include the 'miss' part. And by that, I mean that '*Ms. Janine*' was one of her words, and '*apple*' was the other one…and oh yeah, *'like'*…she says that now, too." He paused for but a second then added, "Somehow, some way, you managed to do what therapists have been trying to do for my baby for the past two years."

"For real?"

"Yeah."

53

Janine was in awe. She'd enjoyed herself as she'd played with little Lisa yesterday. But she hadn't known that their playtime had had such a positive impact on the precious angel. "Wow," she said.

"Yeah, wow."

The wheels in Nate's brain were turning at turbo speed as he reflected on the entire situation. Then he suddenly had an idea. "Ms. Grey, I hate to impose on you — and feel free to tell me no if you want to — but do you think you could spend more quality time with my daughter? I'd pay you, of course. Maybe during the workday, you could spend a couple of hours with her instead of working on design projects. Or if you don't wanna do that, maybe you could spend a few hours with her after work. I know this is spur of the moment, but—,"

"Of course, I can." Janine had a big heart, and she couldn't imagine telling her boss no. Plus, everything in Janine wanted to help the little girl if she could. That's because in Janine's eyes, Lisa really was a sweetie pie, so she had a strong urge to see her flourish and blossom. On top of that, something in Janine's spirit was telling her to say yes. She smiled. "We can start today if you'd like me to. I'm actually a little bit ahead on the designs for the young adult furniture line. I was gonna email you what I have so you can give me your input, so you can tell me if I'm on the right track or not."

Pleased, he grinned, too. "Excellent. How about you head back to your office and email me.

Two Heart's Unspoken Prayers

Then meet me downstairs at the daycare center in ten minutes. We can go from there." He turned his grin up a notch. "And thank you, Ms. Grey…and I mean that from the very bottom of my heart."

"You're welcome, Mr. Blackstone. Lisa's a sweetheart, so it would be my pleasure."

*****

Two Hours Later:

Neither Nate nor Janine had wanted to push it, so, they'd settled on her spending exactly two hours with Lisa. When Janine had walked into a private little alcove of the daycare center a couple of hours ago, she hadn't been quite sure of what to do or what to expect. But she had prayed on everything and asked God to lead her. She ended up making figures with string with Lisa, about like she'd done the previous day when she'd been waiting for Nate to come back to his office. The pair also doodled on sketch paper together using crayons and colored pencils. By the time their two hours were up, Lisa had another word in her vocabulary: sun.

Janine looked down at her Smart Watch. She smiled. "Well, Lisa… Ms. Janine has had a whole bunch of fun with you today, but it's time for me to get back to work upstairs. I plan on coming to see you down here again tomorrow." She paused and added. "That's if it's okay with you."

Janine was rewarded with a hug in answer and that melted her heart.

The two of them heard a deep chuckle behind them, then the words, "I'm guessing that hug means yes."

Janine's eyes met her boss's — he'd just come into the room without her knowledge. She grinned at him and then at Lisa as she, Janine, pulled back from their embrace. "I'll take that as a yes, too," Janine said. "What do you think, Lisa?"

The child simply nodded her head. Then she got back to doodling.

Five minutes later, Lisa was back in her office on the third floor. She looked up and said, "Come in," when someone knocked on her door. It was her boss, Mr. Blackstone.

Nate was all smiles. How could he not be? He had seen evidence that his little girl's interactions with the sista sitting in front of him were working. "Your grandmother was right, Ms. Grey... You definitely have a knack with kids like my daughter. She actually told me goodbye when I just left her with Mrs. Reed in the daycare a few minutes ago. She had never told me hello or goodbye. You're something special. A real blessing."

Janine couldn't help but blush. "I promise you...I'm not doing anything special. I'm just being myself."

He believed her. He believed that she was actually just being herself, but at the same time, he knew there was something extra special about Janine Grey. Yes, she was easy on the eyes — gorgeous really, and he couldn't help noticing that — but she also had a genuine quality about herself that he was sure his daughter was picking up on and reacting to.

He grinned. "Well, I just wanted to come by and personally say thank you... Thank you from the very bottom of my heart."

"You're welcome, boss. The pleasure's all mine. Like I said, Lisa's a sweetheart." She meant it.

CHAPTER NUMBER SIX

"Hey, girl. You didn't call me to tell me how week number two went at your new job, so I figured I'd call you and get a rundown."

Instead of just having a voice call, Janine pressed the button on her cell phone to turn her call into a video session, then she smiled at her bestie as LaVonda's face appeared in living color on her phone screen. "Hey, Vonda. Sorry for not reaching out, honey. I've been super busy...but in the good kinda way."

LaVonda raised an eyebrow. "What? Last week you were grumbling about your self-righteous boss and telling me that you thought that taking that job was a mistake after all. What done happened in a few days to change everything? Turn all that around?"

Janine didn't have to think hard about that one. She sighed and said, "Well, first thing, I had it all wrong about Nate Blackstone. I guess he decided to start thinking about my qualifications, because when I had my first meeting with him the beginning of this week, he told me that my work was outstanding, even though I didn't have a lot of experience." She shook her head as she added, "He wasn't talking none of that mess about me being underqualified."

"Well, amen to that."

"Yep, amen to that."

"But something tells me there's more to it. Spill that tea all over the floor, boo…" Vonda laughed. "Tell me what else good is going on at your job." A knowing look suddenly appeared in Vonda's eyes, and she said, "Oh, wait a minute. I think I got it all wrong. You met somebody, didn't you? Lord have mercy. What's his name, Janine?"

Janine grimaced. "Girl, I meant what I said when I told you I'm not interested in finding nobody right now." She shook her head. "I don't know if I'm ever gonna be interested in going there again. I might've changed my job and the city I live in, but ain't nothing else changed, honey…and I intend on keeping it that way."

Vonda had to admit to herself that she was disappointed to hear her bestie speak those words. She'd been praying for God to step in and touch her girl's heart because she didn't want to see it turn to stone. Vonda had witnessed one too many of her friends and loved ones who'd had that happen to them. After a string of particularly brutal breakups, her friends and loved ones had given up on romance altogether.

"Please don't tell me about getting back out there," Janine warned. "I know you mean well, but I'm really not interested in hearing it, Vonda."

Vonda sighed. "Okay, honey. I won't go there." She turned her lips up in a tiny smile. "But you can still tell me what else good is happening at your job. Something tells me there's a whole lot more than you just making up with your boss."

Janine finally smiled again, too. "Well, there *is* more. Nate…um, Mr. Blackstone, he has a daughter. She's four years old, but she's autistic and for the most part, non-verbal — about like Cameron was when he was her age. It just so happens that I was supposed to meet Mr. Blackstone in his office on Tuesday morning, but his daughter was sitting in there alone. I played with her for about five minutes, and by the time we were done interacting, she knew a new word and was happy to let the whole wide world hear her say it." She chuckled. "Bottom line, Mr. Blackstone wants me to work with her a couple of hours per day… You know, to see if I can help increase her vocabulary, the number of words that she speaks. It was so awesome to be able to work with Lisa — that's her name — because you know how much I love helping others in that way…especially kids."

Vonda definitely knew how her bestie loved helping others. In fact, it had surprised her when Janine had decided to choose a major in the design field instead of one in social work or something similar. So, she couldn't stop herself from hitting her girl back with, "Wow, honey. That's great. At this new gig of yours, you're gonna get to do two of your favorite things — practically at the same time. I can see why you sounded over-the-moon happy when you answered your phone. I'll add little Lisa's name to my prayer list. Hopefully, by the time you're done with her, her parents won't be able to quiet her down." She giggled.

Janine doubted that was gonna happen — at least not anytime soon anyway. But since she understood that with God, all things were possible, she shrugged her shoulder, grinned at her girl, and said, "Thanks honey. Keep us in prayer."

Janine only talked to Vonda for five minutes more. When the two friends finally disconnected their call, Lisa sat down on her sofa and laid her head back against the cushions. She hadn't heard Nate Blackstone mention a Mrs. Blackstone. *I wonder what's the deal with Lisa's mom.*

She only pondered on that a few seconds more, because honestly, she figured it was none of her business. The man wanted her to interact with his daughter — not get all involved in his personal life. She shook her head. That was it for that.

*****

Two Hours Later:

Janine was on the cereal aisle, reaching on the top shelf for a box of her favorite cereal bars, when she felt something gently bump against her legs, then felt small arms wrap around them. She looked down in confusion, only to find Lisa hugging her. Within seconds, she heard Nate Blackstone say, "Oh, sweetie pie. Daddy wasn't expecting you to run off like that."

He bent down and swooped his daughter up, placing her on his hip. Then his eyes met Lisa's and he added, "I'm sorry, Ms. Grey. I guess she must've seen you before I did. And then she took off running. Like I said, I'm sorry." He grinned.

It was unusual for Lisa to grin at anyone — or even make eye contact — but she did both as she looked at Janine and treated her to a shy, little smile. Then she lowered her eyes and said, "Ms. Janine."

Even though the child had dropped her gaze and was now staring at the floor, Janine smiled, too, as she said, "That's right, Lisa…I'm Ms. Janine. And how are you doing today, sweetheart?" She gently tugged one of the little girl's braids to get her attention. "I love your hairstyle, it's so pretty. Did your daddy give you your apple already today?"

That was the magic word because Lisa treated Janine to a giggle. Then she said, "Apple."

Lisa laughed, too. She winked an eye. "Something tells me that he did."

Nate nodded his head. "Yep. We had apple slices this morning for breakfast…the red Honeycrisp ones that you really like…huh, Pumpkin?"

Lisa nodded. "Apple." Then she pointed at Lisa's pocket. "String?"

"Yep," Janine said as she pulled the length of string they'd been playing with all week from out of her pocket. It wasn't supposed to be there. But something had told her to bring it with her that afternoon — she suspected that the *something* had been God. She was happy she'd listened.

Janine smiled again. "String. Yep, I have it with me."

Nate knew what his daughter wanted. But he didn't want to impose on Janine in her off time. So, he said, "You and Ms. Janine can play with the string when we go back to the daycare on Monday, Pumpkin. That'll be in two days." He held up two fingers for emphasis. "Two days. One. Two. We don't wanna bother Ms. Janine in her free time. I'm sure she probably has a whole lotta stuff that she has to take care of today."

The majority of autistic children had problems with expressing their emotions — good and bad emotions both — so Janine knew it was quite the accomplishment when she witnessed the sad look that suddenly materialized on Lisa's cute little face. Janine wanted to reinforce Lisa's expression of her emotions, and she suspected that actually spending a little quality time with the child — right then and there — would aid in that task. That's what prompted Janine to shake her head and say, "Nope. I don't have a lot of things to do right now. I took care of the majority of my chores this morning. If it's okay with your dad, there's a sandwich shop right beside this grocery store. I don't mind spending a little time in there with you after I pay for the things in my cart."

Nate was convinced he knew why his new employee had just said what she had. And he appreciated her for it. Lisa's therapist had emphasized just last week that whenever he, Nate, noticed Lisa making progress, he should act on it asap and encourage it. The specialist had said that doing that would help the newly learned behavior stick in his little girl's brain.

"What do you say, proud papa?" Janine winked an eye. "Are we gonna stop by the sandwich shop?"

He really wanted to, he just had to be sure he and Lisa weren't going to be a nuisance — he had to make sure that Janine wasn't just being nice. "Are you sure we won't be imposing, Ms. Grey?"

"Absolutely positive."

He grinned. "Well, okay then. We'll meet you at the sandwich shop."

Nate had thought they would only be spending ten or fifteen minutes sitting down in the restaurant, they ended up being in there almost a whole hour. To him, it looked as if Janine didn't really want to leave but he was starting to feel guilty, so he had finally said, "Well, Pumpkin... I think we should go ahead and let Ms. Janine enjoy the rest of her Saturday. We'll get to see her again on Monday, God willing. She's already given us an hour of her time." He had smiled at Janine as he added, "And we're really grateful for that."

Janine grinned right back. She affectionately tugged one of Lisa's braids. "Oh, it was my pleasure."

Two Heart's Unspoken Prayers

Now that he and his daughter were in his SUV, heading back home, Nate had thoughts of Janine on his mind. It amazed him that she had chosen to give so selflessly of herself for his child. At first, he'd thought that maybe she was doing it because she wanted to get close to him — hit on him if you will. Nate wasn't the type of person who tooted his own horn, but he'd had lots of women try to get with him because they assumed he was an eligible bachelor. He knew that the fact that he owned a very successful business — one that came with a matching high salary — made him even more desirable in some women's eyes. A target even.

But as Nate had spent time with Janine earlier that day, he could tell that she wasn't interested in him at all. Her entire focus had been on Lisa.

It was a little ridiculous to him, but he suddenly felt a little sad about that. He shook his head. *You tripping, bruh.*

Hours later, after he'd finally gotten Lisa to bed, he was sitting in his den watching a little television and thoughts of Janine invaded his mind once more.

Maybe I've been single for too long. That's what he thought to himself. *Maybe thoughts like this start happening after a brotha like myself hasn't been on a date in over three years.*

Convinced that he was right in his self-reflection, he pushed all thoughts of Janine from his mind. He turned the channel and started watching the baseball game. As far as he was concerned, that was it for that.

*****

Across Town:

When she was a little girl and a teenager, Janine used to journal. She had dropped the habit as a young adult, but after the debacle with Jermaine, she'd picked it back up because journaling had always made her reflect on herself and her reality. So, journaling was now a regular part of her life again, it was a daily thing for her.

Every night, before going to bed, she would pull out her journal and begin writing. And that's exactly what she was doing right now. Snuggled into a corner of her sofa with a soothing cup of lavender tea, she held a pen in her hand while thinking about what she wanted to write.

Her mind began reflecting over her day. The most prominent thing that had happened to her was her run-in with Lisa and her father. Janine knew that their little rendezvous was exactly what she wanted to write about. She began jotting down her thoughts about Lisa, but then her mind roved over to Nate Blackstone, causing her to stop writing. She began thinking about her boss instead.

He's a good father. Lisa is blessed to have him in her life. She grimaced when her brain began focusing on all of Nate Blackstone's physical attributes. His smooth brown skin, his strong chin, his prominent jawline, his deep, sultry-yet-kind eyes.

She shook her head. *I need to quit. I bet that conversation with Vonda this morning is what's got me sitting in here thinking about ol' boy like that. Vonda kept hinting at me needing to look for a boyfriend... I bet that's why I got how good-looking Nate Blackstone is on my mind. I'm sure of it.*

She hmphed. "Get thee behind me Satan. I'm rebuking you in the Holy name of Jesus, 'cause the devil is a lie." That's what she whispered under her breath. She didn't have time to entertain no thoughts like that.

She sighed and closed her journal. Then she took her shower, said her prayers, and retired for the night.

CHAPTER NUMBER SEVEN

Two Hours Later:

It seemed like it was part of her dream, but something was telling Janine that the loud beeping sound she was hearing was part of reality. She was super groggy, but she began to slowly open her eyes.

As her lids lifted, she began to feel a stinging sensation behind them, and it took her only half a second to realize a burning smell was assaulting her nostrils. Then she began to cough from the apparent irritation that the air in her bedroom was causing her.

That's smoke I'm smelling... Something's on fire! That's what finally registered in her brain, causing her to jump out of bed.

She quickly pushed her feet into a pair of sneakers, grabbed her cell phone, and dashed to her front door. She reached for the doorknob but immediately pulled her hand back from the hot metal. *The fire's right outside my door! That's why the knob's hot!*

For safety reasons, Janine had considered trying to find a second-story apartment when she'd first moved there to Durham — that's because she'd always thought upper-story apartments were less susceptible to break-ins. But now, she was happy that the only thing that had been available in her price range had been a ground-level unit.

She made a quick dash to the double patio doors at the back of her kitchen and rushed outside.

Her first thought was to start banging on her neighbor's doors, but she had to drag air into her slightly smoke-filled lungs before she could manage that. After about a half minute of lying on the cold cement of her patio, breathing as deep as she could, she finally dragged herself up and began banging on doors and shouting, "Get out now! Fire!!!"

As she heard the wail of sirens approaching in the distance, Janine didn't think she had ever been so happy to hear emergency personnel on their way.

*****

Across Town:

Nate couldn't get to sleep, and he was tired of trying. Normally, he made it to Dreamland within ten minutes of his head hitting his ergonomically correct, doctor-approved pillow. But not tonight. He'd been lying there for a whole hour thinking of some of everything under the sun. However, a whole lot of his thoughts had been about his newest employee — Janine.

He didn't understand why he couldn't get her off his mind.

He shook his head and decided to go to the kitchen and brew himself a cup of the specialty tea that his sister had gifted him for Christmas — she said it was called Sleepytime or something or another. He couldn't remember the name; all he could remember was the tea's purported function. And he certainly needed some sleepy time tonight. That's because instead of going to the regular eleven o'clock service at his church, he'd told his pastor that he would be filling a pew for the morning service — the one that started at eight-thirty. That meant he and Lisa needed to be out of the house by 8:05 at the latest.

He figured that the only thing he had working in his favor was the fact that Lisa never complained about him getting her dressed in the mornings. She was quiet, but she was always cooperative. He suspected it had something to do with the bright colors that he made sure her clothes came in. His little girl loved shades on the bold side of the color spectrum.

A little under ten minutes later, with his cup of tea in hand, he made his way back to his study. He grabbed the remote and turned the television on. He was channel surfing until he landed on the local station. The face he saw on the screen was very familiar — and not because the person was a news reporter. It was because he had just been with the woman less than ten hours ago.

Nate frowned. *Janine's on the news. What in the world is going on?* He could tell from the headline at the bottom of the screen that there had been a fire at an apartment complex in the city. But he didn't really need to see the headline to understand what had happened. The firefighters who were still active at the scene, and the thick black smoke billowing from one of the apartment buildings, told him what was going on.

He turned up the volume so he could hear what Janine was saying. She looked distressed as she told the reporter about how she had been awakened by her fire alarm going off and had rushed out of her apartment to safety. When the reporter asked her where she would be living now that her apartment had been burnt down, she had sadly shaken her head and said, "I don't know. I'm hoping that the Red Cross or somebody can step in and help me and the other occupants who lost everything. This is a terrible situation that we're in. The only good thing about it is that God blessed everybody to make it out in time…even the pets."

Nate felt sorry for everything that the sista with the big heart on his television screen had gone through. He had a sudden urge to help her because the sad, devastated look in her eyes was tearing at his soul. And he knew exactly what he could do to help her best.

He took his cup of tea into the kitchen and poured it down the drain. Then he went to his bedroom and pulled a pair of jeans and a t-shirt from out his closet. He activated his Bluetooth and told his phone to call Ayanna. Ayanna was his younger sister, and she didn't go to bed until three or four o'clock every morning. He had a favor to ask of her and he was more than certain she would be willing to oblige.

"Hey big brother...mom and dad okay?" Those were the first words out of Ayanna's mouth because Nate was normally fast asleep at eleven o'clock at night. She couldn't imagine him calling her close to midnight unless something was wrong.

Reaching into the top drawer of his dresser and pulling out his car keys he said, "Yeah they're just fine, Ayanna. I talked to them both earlier this evening. But I have a big favor to ask of you. Can you be over here at my place in ten minutes? Lisa's sleep, but I need you to watch her for me. I have to make a run real quick. I don't think I'mma be out long. I'm hoping that I'll be back home within an hour."

Seeing that they lived in the same subdivision, Ayanna's condo was only a one-minute drive away from her brother's house. So she said, "Sure thing, bro. Give me five minutes to get there." She laughed. "Don't tell me you got the late-night munchies and you running out to a fast-food joint... What happened to the intermediate fasting thing that you were telling me you wanted to try out?"

"Oh, it's not that." He sighed. "A fire just broke out over at the Cardinal Slope apartments. A friend of mine stays there. I just saw her on the news. Unfortunately, she's been burnt out of her home. I wanted to head over there to see what I can do to help her out. You know, to offer my assistance."

"Oh no." Ayanna began scanning her brain, trying to figure out which one of her brother's friends had been affected by the unfortunate incident. When she came up empty-handed, she finally asked, "Who do we know who lives over there? Who got burnt outta their apartment?"

Nate shook his head. "You haven't met her yet. She's the new employee at Blackstone Manufacturing that I was telling you about — the one who's really good with Lisa. The one who's been helping me expand her vocabulary this week. Her name's Janine. She doesn't have any friends or family here in Durham, so she's all alone in all of this. She could use some support just about now."

Ayanna frowned. "Okay, Nate. I'll be over there at your place in a few. You can go ahead and make your way out to your car if you want to. By the time you're backing out, I'll probably be pulling in. I'm about to put my shoes on. Prayers for everyone involved."

*****

Fifteen minutes later, Nate was pulling into Janine's apartment complex. He was hoping and praying she was still there, and it just so happened that his prayer was answered. He saw her within seconds of pulling his SUV into a parking spot located just far enough from the commotion that he wouldn't be in the way of the ongoing firefighting efforts.

When she heard someone calling her name, Janine had been about to make a phone call to the Red Cross hotline. One of the news crew members had handed her a card with the charity's number printed on it. Confused, she looked up from her cell phone and squinted her eyes to see who was calling out to her. The voice sounded familiar, but in her current state — and because of all the noise going on around her — she couldn't quite make a connection to a face. As soon as she saw Nate standing there, she scrunched her eyes together in surprise. Why surprise? Well, the apartment complex she was living in wasn't rundown or anything — it was average — but she hadn't figured that an executive with bank — like her boss — lived there. She pictured him living in a big ol' mini-mansion in some nice suburb on the outskirts of the city.

"Nate…um, I mean Mr. Blackstone, were you burnt out, too?"

He shook his head. "No. I live on the other side of town. I just so happened to be up watching the late-night news and I saw you giving your interview. I hopped in my car and drove over here because I wanted to help you out." He shook his head. "Not *wanted,* as in past tense. But I *want* to help you out, Janine…as in right now."

She thought that was really nice of him to come over and make his offer, but she really didn't know what he could do for her, and she shared with him as much.

Nate listened patiently, then he said, "Yeah, I understand where you're coming from, but I actually have a proposition that I'd like to make to you…one that I figure both of us could benefit from." He smiled. "Well, actually all three of us."

Yep, she was definitely confused now. "Okay. Um…who's the three of us?"

"Me, you, and Lisa." He paused for but a second then added, "My mother is Lisa's normal babysitter, but like I told you the other day, she's on a cruise right now and she won't be back for another three weeks or so. Lisa hates interruptions in her schedule, and if I'm being honest about it, she really doesn't enjoy being at the daycare center — even though it's a nice facility, and it's a nice environment for your average child. My house is big — much larger than what Lisa and I need for ourselves. In fact, I've been considering downsizing for some time now, I just hadn't gotten around to doing it yet."

Realizing that he was being long-winded, and that she was probably tired and still traumatized, he offered up a tiny smile of support and said, "What I'm trying to say is, I can offer you a room at my house and you could babysit Lisa for me and work with her on her vocabulary. You've only interacted with her a handful of days, and my baby's already saying twice the number of words that she's said in the past two years. So, yeah, Lisa would win if you spent more time with her...I just know it. And you would have somewhere comfortable and friendly to live at...you know, until you get your housing situation straightened out."

Like Nate, Janine suspected that Lisa would benefit from having her around. But that didn't negate the fact that she already had a nine-to-five that she'd committed to. "What about my job at Blackstone?"

He smiled. "I figured you'd say that. I have an answer to that one, too. You could work remotely... You know, work from home until my mom gets back and takes over with my baby girl full-time. I even have a drafting table in my basement, and all the materials and software that you could possibly need to complete your designs."

Janine hadn't really wanted to go to a shelter or a hotel, so her boss's offer sounded like a Godsend. Normally, she probably would've said: *Let me go home and think on it...lemme pray about it.* But she didn't have a home to go to. So, she simply smiled, thanked God for sending her a blessing and said, "Alright, Mr. Blackstone. Thank you."

Nate believed in an old saying that the mothers and fathers at his church frequently used. And that saying was: *It's a blessing to be a blessing.* So, pleased with Janine's acceptance of his offer, he grinned and said, "You're very welcome."

Two Heart's Unspoken Prayers

She turned slightly to the left and frowned at her apartment. "I would ask you to give me a second to grab some things, but everything I own went up in flames in that fire. I guess the only good thing about it is that I have some of my really important stuff — like some of my photo albums and mementos — stashed away in my parents' garage. When I moved up here, I only wanted to pay for one U-Haul truck. The stuff that didn't fit in it, I kept in Georgia."

He nodded. "Well, we can thank God for small mercies then."

"Yeah. I suppose so." She grimaced. "I can't even drive my car over to your place because my keys are still in the apartment. When I smelled that smoke, I pretty much hit the ground running."

He swept his hand in a gracious waving motion. He smiled. "Your chariot is my chariot, Janine. My car is right over there."

She hesitated for several seconds, but she finally returned his smile with one of her own and said, "Thanks."

*****

Instead of heading straight to his house, Nate drove them to the local Target, where Janine picked up a couple hundred dollars' worth of necessities. Nate paid for it all since Janine's credit cards and cash were lost in the fire. She'd insisted on Nate letting her give him an IOU, or deducting the money from her paycheck, but he'd countered by insisting that she allow him to buy her the things as a gift.

Tired from everything that had happened to her that evening, Janine conceded defeat somewhere close to the cleaning supplies aisle. However, she vowed to herself that she would find some type of way to reimburse her boss for his kindness.

Surprisingly, they made it back to Nate's home within the one hour that he had initially discussed with his sister. The house that Janine was now staring at matched up in her brain with the type of place she pictured Nate Blackstone living in: A handsome-looking, two-story white brick home in a quaint neighborhood. She suddenly had a concern. His wife.

As soon as he cut the ignition, Janine looked over at him and said, "I shoulda said something before now, but I guess I was too disturbed by everything I just went through with that fire and all—," her eyes met his, "—but what does your wife have to say about all of this? I don't wanna be walking in your home and disrupting your heaven."

He frowned. "I'm not married, Janine. I'm a single dad."

"Oh. Um, okay." She wasn't quite sure about what to think about that. But she was kinda tired, so she figured she would give it some thought in the morning.

Two Heart's Unspoken Prayers

He unlocked the SUV doors and they both stepped outside into the warm, summer night. Janine was intending on getting her bags herself, but she was moving kind of slow, which gave Nate the opportunity to collect all five of her bags and smile at her. "I got 'em, Janine. You look exhausted. I can give you a tour of the house tonight if you want to, but if you prefer to wait until the morning, that would be OK with me, too. Like I told you on the drive over, I have several laptops you can use in the house. I'll bring one to the guest room so you can get back started on doing whatever you need to do." He chuckled. "I know most of us would be lost without our computers."

She couldn't help but smile at that because she had definitely grabbed her cell phone before she ran out of her burning apartment.

They stepped into Nate's spacious foyer. Despite being tired, Janine couldn't help but admire the space — she figured it was the designer in her. The foyer was decorated in soothing shades of blue and brown with accents of green. She really liked it.

"All the bedrooms are upstairs," he said as he guided his guest towards the staircase. But they didn't make it there because Nate's sister, Ayanna, walked out the study, squealed and said, "Oh my Lord, DesignSistah2000?! I can't believe it's you!"

Janine wasn't used to hearing people outside of the internet referring to her by her YouTube channel handle. But when she glanced over towards the double doors that she assumed led to Nate's study, her eyes lit up and she, in return, squealed, "YannaTheBlingQueen?!"

All Nate could do was stand back with a curious expression on his face as his sister and his new nanny/furniture designer/house guest gave each other a hug.

He smirked. "I take it the two of you know each other?"

The ladies pulled back grinning. Ayanna said, "Uh, yeah. But online only. We both have YouTube channels. And we friended each other and follow each other online."

Janine nodded her head in agreement. "Yep. And since both of our channels are about design and home decor, we even talked about doing a few joint episodes together. But we hadn't gotten around to doing that yet." She looked over at Nate. "You gave me my new job and I kinda dropped my YouTube channel for a while so I could focus all my energy on work."

Still smiling, Ayanna said, "This is so awesome. I guess we're gonna have a chance to do a couple of videos together after all. But instead of being virtual, we can do 'em in person."

"Definitely."

"Thank God the Lord let you make it out that fire practically unscathed." Ayanna grimaced. "The news station is still doing live coverage of the situation. It's still burning in some spots. It's a blessing there were no causalities...just property loss. Property can be replaced—," she shook her head, "—but people can't. Know what I mean?"

Nate and Janine nodded in agreement. They definitely understood what she was talking about.

"Well—," Ayanna said, "—it's going on one. I'mma gon' head and bounce myself on home. I'll talk to you guys later." She turned to Janine. "Welcome to North Carolina, DesignSistah2000." She blushed. "What's your for-real first name again? My big brother here told me what it was before he left to go help you out, but I forgot...sorry, girl. Officially, my name's Ayanna. And you are?"

Janine laughed. "Janine."

Ayanna giggled, too. "Right, see you later, Janine."

After he closed the front door behind his sibling, Nate turned to his houseguest and smiled. "Well, now that the reunion is over with, I guess I'd better show you to your room."

Janine could do nothing but agree. She'd been through the wringer. She was tired.

CHAPTER NUMBER EIGHT

It felt odd waking up in a different bed that morning, but Janine was happy for it. She knew she had been blessed to open her eyes at all.

The authorities still weren't letting anyone into their damaged apartments. According to the special agent Janine had talked to five minutes ago on the phone, they were guessing that she would be able to go take a look at her apartment the following day.

Janine understood that most — if not all of her things would be smoke damaged, and thus not be salvageable. But she still wanted to see if there was anything she could reclaim, anything she could save.

She was surprised that her eyes had cracked themselves open at seven o'clock that morning, which meant she'd only gotten five and a half hours of sleep. But since her body had woken itself up naturally, she figured she was going to just go with it...she wasn't gonna try to sleep in.

The guest room that Nate was loaning her was actually a second master bedroom — at least as far as Janine was concerned, it was.

The room was large, and it had its own full bathroom. It even had a little alcove that was a perfect little sitting space. She was more than sure she was going to enjoy her three weeks living there.

Two Heart's Unspoken Prayers

She didn't know how her day was going to play out, but she figured that she needed to go ahead and take her shower and get dressed. Twenty minutes later, she was rocking a pair of comfortable purple sweatpants and a t-shirt and heading downstairs to find her boss's kitchen.

It didn't take a lot of effort to find it though. She simply allowed her nose to lead her to the back of the house, the area where the delicious aromas of breakfast were coming from.

"Good morning," she said to Nate as she spied him crisping bacon and sausages at the stove.

He looked over his shoulder and grinned. "Morning, Janine. I generally go all out for breakfast on Sunday mornings. I'm doing bacon, sausage, toast, hash browns, eggs… You gotta let me know how you want your eggs done. Easy over, scrambled, hard-boiled, omelet…I'm ya man." He winked an eye. "I can handle all of that and then some. So, how you want 'em? Your eggs?"

His energy was contagious. She couldn't help but grin. "Whatever type is easiest for you. Thank you, Chef Blackstone," she kidded, garnering a chuckle from Nate. She then smiled at Lisa, who was sitting at the kitchen island. "Good morning, Lisa. Have you had your apple yet?"

Without looking up from her plate, Lisa said, "Yes. Apple."

Janine sat down at the island beside Lisa and began drawing on the sketchpad she'd slipped in her pocket before coming downstairs. Yep, she'd suspected that if she ran into Lisa, she'd need it. "Okay, sweetheart… What about milk? Did you have milk, too?"

Janine pushed the sketchpad along the island top and got it close enough to Lisa so that the little girl could see the image of a glass of milk she'd quickly drawn. "Milk, Lisa. The milk looks yummy in the glass in this picture, doesn't it? Do you wanna feel it?"

The little girl didn't reach out to touch the drawing like Janine had hoped she'd do. But she did something that was just as good. She said, "Milk. Yummy milk."

Janine chuckled. "Yep. I think milk is yummy, too, sweetie pie."

Standing at that stove scrambling eggs, Nate felt his heart bursting with pride. His baby girl had two new words in her repertoire: yummy and milk.

"There're plates in that cabinet right behind you, Janine. If you wanna grab one, you can help yourself to breakfast." He pointed to his left. "And of course, there's coffee, and the mugs are in the cabinet beside the plates. And there's juice in the frigid."

"Apple," Lisa said.

Janine and Nate both chuckled.

"Yep," Nate said. "We also have apples."

The three of them sat there and ate breakfast together that morning. When they were almost done eating, Nate looked over at Janine and said, "Like I told you last night, you're welcome to come to church with Lisa and I this morning."

Janine shook her head. "Thanks for the invite, but I'mma have to decline." A wistful expression appeared in her eyes. "But it's mighty tempting though. Back in Atlanta, I went to services every Sunday…and Bible study at least twice a month on Wednesdays. I kinda miss that. There's nothing like worship service. It renews you, builds you up to face another week. Know what I mean?"

Nate knew exactly what she meant. That's why he made it a point to be up in the house of the Lord most Sundays. "I always get a blessing when I go to service at Temple of Deliverance… There's probably one waiting there for you, too." He smiled.

Janine sighed. "I know that I'm new to the city and I only know a handful of people here, but if I roll up in church with you and Lisa, people's tongues are gonna probably get to wagging. I might end up really liking your church. I don't wanna give out the wrong impression or get people talking about me before I even get up in there good. You understand where I'm coming from?"

Hearing it that way made him understand completely. He smiled. "Okay, gotcha. My mama always told me that men are slow and dense sometimes." He laughed. "I think I just now realize what she meant by that."

Janine turned her lips up, too. "Your mother sounds like a really smart lady, boss. It'll be nice to meet her."

Something told Nate that his mom would enjoy meeting Janine, too. In many ways, they seemed like they were kindred spirits. Janine had a welcoming, friendly aura about herself…an aura similar to his mother's.

"Well, they have a live recording of the service, and they broadcast it on YouTube—," he grinned again, "—based on the fact that you have your very own YouTube channel, I'm more than sure you know how that works."

"Yep."

"Maybe you can check them out."

She nodded her head. "I think I'll do that, Mr. Blackstone."

Hearing her call him *Mr. Blackstone* didn't sit right with Nate. To him, it seemed as if he and Lisa were building a friendship. *Mr. Blackstone* didn't feel like it had a place in their mutual communications — especially not in his house, while they were sitting down at his kitchen table having a very enjoyable conversation.

"What's wrong?" she asked, sensing something was amiss because of the look that was now on his face.

He began pinching his chin using his thumb and his index finger. "Well, I was kinda hoping you could call me Nate — at least when we're not at Blackstone Manufacturing. You calling me Mr. Blackstone just sounds so formal." He waved a hand around his kitchen table. "And the situation

we're currently having just isn't formal like that."
His eyes met hers. "Know what I mean, Janine?"

She'd actually had to stop herself from
allowing the name *Nate* to roll off her tongue a
couple of times in the past two days, so, she knew
exactly what he was getting at. She even knew
she'd already slipped up and called him by his first
name a time or two since yesterday.

She grinned. "Okay, Nate." She winked. "I
understand you perfectly. Mr. Blackstone works at
Blackstone Manufacturing. Nate lives here at
home."

He chuckled. "Now that sounds about right."

*****

An hour later, Janine was home alone at
Nate's place while he and Lisa were at church.
Since he'd fixed breakfast for her, Janine had
insisted that he allow her to do the dishes and clean
up the kitchen, which she was doing now as she
listened to the live broadcast of Nate's church
service on the laptop he'd loaned her.

Concentrating on the sermon that the pastor
was delivering, Janine had to admit to herself that
Nate had been right: She loved his church. She was
certain she would be attending an upcoming service
in person. But like she'd explained to her boss,
she'd be going there alone. The church had a
medium-sized congregation — she could see about
two-hundred or so parishioners on the computer

screen. She figured she would be able to slip in, take a seat, blend in with the crowd and enjoy herself.

After the service ended its live stream on her laptop, Janine looked at the clock, hoping that she had enough time to call Vonda before her girl headed out to the eleven-a.m. service that she normally attended back in Atlanta. It was only five till ten, so, Janine picked up her cell phone and dialed her bestie's number.

"Hey, Janine…everything okay up there in North Carolina?"

Janine sighed, then she proceeded to tell Vonda about the housefire.

"What?! Your placed burned down to the ground? Are you okay, boo?"

Janine had been expecting the concern, if the tables had been turned, she would've felt the same way. "Yeah, I'm fine. I had a little cough right afterwards, but that went away overnight while I was sleep."

"And where you staying? A shelter?"

"No," she smiled, "I actually spent the night at Nate's place, he—"

Janine couldn't finish her sentence because her girl interrupted her with a quickness by asking, "Nate, as in your boss Nate? Nate Blackstone?"

"Yep. He was looking at the news last night and he saw the news person interviewing me about the fire. I wasn't expecting it — it came right out the blue — but he drove over there, found me, and offered me a room at his place. He even took me to Target and bought me some things to replace some of the stuff that I lost." She smiled. "He said it's a blessing to be a blessing."

"Wow, that's amazing. I know how much you hate staying in motels and hotels. So that really was a blessing. It's a good thing that his wife is nice like that. A lot of wives wouldn't want to open their homes to a complete stranger." She paused for but a second then added, "Well, you're not really a complete stranger. You're his employee. And yeah, you've only been there working for him a few weeks, but you guys communicate a lot, and you work kind of close together, right?"

Janine wasn't sure which part of her girl's comment to address first. She decided to start at the bottom and work her way back up to the top. "Yes, we work together, and like I was telling you, I've been working one on one with his little girl, helping her to increase her vocabulary. And yes, God has blessed my work with Lisa to be going along phenomenally. And speaking of his little girl, I'm actually gonna be a nanny for her for three or so weeks while his mother is on vacation. Nate and I struck up an agreement where I would do most of my work for the company here at his house while I stay at home with Lisa most of the day. She doesn't really like daycare and having to go there would probably hinder her learning new words each day from me. So, I'm okay with that."

Remembering how fond her girl was of working with children and helping people, Vonda grinned and said, "Even though you lost your stuff in that fire, I guess you're still happy that you're gonna have such an interactive role with that little girl, while still being able to work on your furniture designs, huh?" She chuckled. "Now I know that most parents love their kids and love spending time with them, but I bet your boss's wife is happy that she's about to have a live-in-nanny. What did she say, boo? His wife? She happy or nah?"

Janine shook her head. "Nate doesn't have a wife, Vonda. He's a single dad."

"What?"

"Yeah, he's a single dad…as in it's just him and Lisa. He said it's been that way for a couple of years now."

Vonda drew her eyebrows together. "So, his baby-mama ain't nowhere in the picture?"

"It doesn't seem like she is."

Vonda got to thinking about the situation real hard, scrunching up her face as she did so. She finally said, "Okay…this boss of yours, Nate… How old is he and what does he look like?"

Janine could already tell where her girl was going. She shook her head and cautioned, "You might as well take that thought out your mind right now, LaVonda Marie Patterson. I don't know how old that man is and I ain't focusing on him like that, meaning, I don't care if he's handsome or not." She sucked her teeth. "And he definitely ain't checking for my behind. All he has been to me is nice. Plus, what would it look like…him trying to hit on his employee? He's not that type of man. I can already tell that. He's kind, decent, and upstanding. He's the type of brotha who takes his God and his salvation seriously. He reminds me a lot of your brother, Kevin. You know, *Pastor* Kevin?"

"Alright, boo. No need to get your panties in a bunch. I was just wondering, that's all. What kinda friend would I be if I didn't try to peep the whole situation so I could look out for your best interest?" She smiled. "Just let me know if you need anything and keep me posted. Okay, honey?"

"Okay, Vonda. Thanks."

After finally getting off the phone with her bestie, Janine sat down at Nate's spacious kitchen island and began thinking about the conversation she'd just had with Vonda. *I can't believe my girl actually thought that something could pop off between me and Nate*. She scoffed. *That definitely ain't happening*.

She then began thinking about one of the questions that Vonda had asked her: *What does he look like?* She pulled her eyebrows together and began looking at Nate's face using her mind's eye. She had to admit that he was a good-looking brotha.

She shook her head. *Even if he did step to me — which I know he's not — I wouldn't be, and I ain't interested*.

Nate had good looks, a prosperous career, a bright future ahead of him…all things that Janine's

91

cheating ex, Jermaine, had had going for himself. And Janine had seen how that had turned out for her, how it had hurt her.

She grimaced. *Nate seems like a decent enough dude, but I know for a fact that everything that glitters ain't gold.* She hmphed. *And relationships are for the birds anyways.*

CHAPTER NUMBER NINE

"Hey big brother, I'm just calling to see how things with Janine ended up working out. I would have asked you about it today at church, but I didn't make it to the early morning service like you did. I ended up going to the eleven o'clock one, instead. So, I suppose the two of us missed each other like ships passing in the night." She smiled. But anyways, I know Janine spent the night at your place in your guest room, but did you help her find a decent hotel room after church today?"

Standing on the balcony outside his bedroom window staring up at the stars — something he did many a clear summer night since he moved into his new home a year ago — Nate moved his phone over to his other ear and wished that he had brought his Bluetooth out there with him. "Hold on a sec, sis… let me put you on speaker."

He pressed the speaker icon and said, "Okay, I'm back, and to answer your question, I didn't help Janine find a hotel room. That's because I offered her my guest room for the next three weeks or so — you know, until mom and dad get back from vacation. She's gonna be babysitting and teaching Lisa. Ever since she started interacting with Janine this past week, Lisa's been doing so well in her speech development. You even noticed that yourself. You told me you did when we talked day before yesterday." He chuckled. "I gave Janine a break today though, so she doesn't officially start on the job until tomorrow."

Nate smiled as he thought about how Janine had insisted on helping with Lisa that day anyways. That had been even more evidence to him that she was a good person, that her heart was in the right place. He admired that about her character.

Ayanna grimaced. She knew what she'd just heard her sibling say, she just couldn't believe it. "Come again, Nate."

"I gave Janine a job assisting me with Lisa."

Her brother was usually very careful about who he allowed in his daughter's world, so it surprised Ayanna that he was allowing a woman he had just met weeks earlier to stay with his child practically 24/7. "Wow, big brother," she said, "I realize that I kinda/sorta know Janine from our online presence, but you barely know her at all. Yet you're letting her keep Lisa." She shook her head. "It's not that I don't trust Janine, mind you, it's just that—"

"I understand where you're coming from, sis. I prayed on it, and God told me that it would be alright. Plus, you know I did a thorough background check on Janine before I hired her at Blackstone Manufacturing. I do that for all the employees I bring on board at my business. There were zero red flags, and I checked all her references — or rather

Donovan did, but that's basically the same thing as me doing it myself. God blessed me with a great vice president in that one, and an even better friend. Bottom line, she checks out."

Ayanna grinned. "Well, I suppose she does. It's just that I was a little surprised, that's all. You have it on the highest authority that it's okay — the Lord himself — so I'mma leave it alone."

Acknowledging his sister's words, Nate nodded his head. "God is all in this, sis. I can feel it. In fact, you know I normally go to bed by 10:30, and I'm usually asleep by eleven. How about last night, I just couldn't get to sleep for some reason? And I mean no matter how hard I tried. So, I got up, fixed me a cup of that Sleepytime tea that you gifted me last Christmas, and started watching television. Eventually, I ended up on the local news channel, where I saw Janine talking to a reporter about how she was alone in the city and had just lost everything."

He frowned, then shook his head. "I'm certain it wasn't a coincidence that things played out like that. I know it was God who wouldn't allow me to get to sleep. He wanted me to hear Janine say that she was homeless so that I would be inspired to offer her this position so that she could ultimately help my baby out."

He sighed just from thinking about it. "You know how long I've been praying that God would show up, show out, and change things for my little girl. God is telling me in my spirit that he is using

Janine to help Lisa. I'm just a loving parent and willing participant in bringing forth God's will. I'm letting the Master work it all out."

Ayanna was sure that people who didn't have a relationship with Christ wouldn't have understood what her brother was talking about. But being a woman of faith, a sista of conviction, Ayanna did.

She smiled. "Well amen to that, brother dear. You know I love my sweet little niecy-poo with my everything. Anything that the Lord is willing to do to help her thrive and blossom, I'm all for it."

The siblings wrapped up their phone call and Nate was left standing on his balcony alone. That's when he heard someone on the patio below his balcony. Seeing that he had a fenced-in backyard, he knew that no one should have been out there. Fifteen seconds later, he was opening his double patio doors investigating. Turns out it was his houseguest. It was Janine.

Startled, Janine jumped in her seat under the gazebo when she heard the patio doors open. She immediately calmed down when she noticed Nate standing there.

Nate smiled as he joined her on his spacious patio. "I didn't mean to scare you, Janine. I'm sorry."

She placed a hand over her chest and smiled. "My heart only missed two point five beats. But that's okay though, because at my physical this year, my doctor said that my ticker is strong as an ox."

He chuckled. "That's good to know." He looked up at the sky, at the stars, much like he'd been doing before his sister had dialed his phone about ten minutes ago. "Don't tell me that you're a stargazer, too."

Janine looked up at the sky, she smiled. "Only on gorgeous, warm nights like tonight. My grandmother used to stay that the sky is God's tapestry. When I was little, I didn't quite know what she meant. But now that I'm older, I understand. The stars and how they're placed up there in that sky is like a perfect piece of artwork. When a star burns out, or a new one is created, the artwork — the tapestry — changes. But it's beautiful all the same."

He nodded, he grinned. "The night sky as a tapestry...I like that."

"Yeah, me, too. My grandmother's been gone almost ten years now, but I'm so glad that God blessed me to have her in my life the length of time that I did. Grandparents are special... Know what I mean?"

"I sure do, Janine." And he was telling the truth, too. Both sets of his grandparents had helped to mold him into the man he was, the man he always wanted to be.

There was something special about that moment as they stood out there on that patio looking up at the stars. The ambience of it all made

Nate want to share with Janine what God had put on his heart about the reason she'd come into his and Lisa's lives.

"You know, Janine, speaking of blessings, I'm sure God sent you my way so you could be a blessing to my daughter." He sighed. "I've been praying for two long years, praying that God would somehow break the yoke that seems like it's been placed around my daughter's mouth. I believe you're the answer to my prayer. I was just talking to Ayanna on the phone before I came down here. I was telling her how I'm normally in bed and asleep by eleven o'clock. Yet, last night, God allowed me to not be able to get to sleep. I ended up seeing you on the news and you know the rest of the story about how you got here to my house."

Janine didn't doubt what Nate had just told her. Why? Because she knew that God moved in mysterious ways, she understood that the Lord has a strategic plan set out well before any of us even see it.

Lisa had really touched Janine's heart. So, she wanted a breakthrough for the little girl, too. Her eyes met Nate's. "One of my favorite scriptures is Matthew 18:20."

"For where two or three are gathered together in My name, I am there in the midst of them."

She smiled. She nodded. "Yes, that's the one." Surprising him, she held out both her hands towards him. "There's two of us here right now. Let's pray on it, Nate."

Always the believer in the power of prayer, he could do nothing but take Janine's hands into his and allow her to pray for his daughter and the journey the three of them were about to undertake.

Their impromptu prayer session only lasted a couple of minutes, and when they were done, they only stayed out there talking on that patio for about five minutes more. Then Nate made his way to his bedroom — it was approaching his bedtime — and Janine did the same.

As he laid in bed that night, working on getting to sleep, Nate had Janine on his mind. Lying there in bed, he smiled because he was imagining her smile in his head.

She's a good woman, Lord. Thank you again for bringing her into my life…into my daughter's life. And she's pretty, too…

He found himself frowning at that last little part. He knew that Janine's physical attributes shouldn't have had a single thing to do with his current train of thought. But he couldn't get her pretty face out his brain.

And the way she tilts her head when she laughs…that's cute. And her—

He frowned again. *Lord, I feel like a schoolboy with a crush on the captain of the cheerleading squad.*

He shook his head, he sighed. Then he forced himself to think about anything and everything but Janine. Fortunately for him, his ploy worked...he finally got to sleep.

CHAPTER NUMBER TEN

Janine smiled at her four-year-old charge and said, "Okay, Lisa… you wanna help me fix lunch?"

Janine and Lisa were sitting at the drafting table in Nate's large, surprisingly bright basement when she'd asked the little girl that question. All things considered, Janine thought that they'd had a great morning together. For half of the morning, Janine had drawn pictures of various household items, and then she and Lisa had colored the pictures together. The other part of the morning was spent going over a photo album that contained snapshots of Nate and his little girl having fun together. Janine wasn't the best portrait artist, but she thought she'd done a decent job of sketching Nate. She and Lisa had colored all of those pictures, too. As they had gone along, Janine had kept emphasizing to the little girl that the man in the pictures was daddy.

And what was Janine hoping to accomplish? She was hoping that eventually, Lisa would begin to address her father by his title: dad, instead of greeting her father with silence and downcast eyes.

Janine wasn't a parent, but she imagined that every parent had a desire to hear their child call them mom or dad. She certainly knew that would be the case if she had a little boy or girl.

Thinking about someday having a child of her own made Janine sad. Deep down in her heart, she wanted to be a wife and a mother. However, the recent events with Jermaine, her ex, had tarnished that vision in her brain. But it was still there. Just soiled and broken. She had to admit that to herself.

She smiled at Lisa and repeated her question. "Wanna go help me make lunch, sweetheart?"

Without looking up, Lisa placed the crayon she'd been using on the table in front of her. She replied, "Apple."

Janine grinned. She gave Lisa a heartfelt little hug. That was good enough of an answer for her.

It was a little after one and Janine was tidying up the kitchen from their lunch when she heard the front door alarm go off, followed by it quickly being deactivated and reactivated. She suspected that it was Nate returning home extremely early. Well, she hoped that was the case because she certainly didn't know who else it could be. Her suspicions were confirmed by him shouting, "It's just me."

Relieved, Janine grinned. "We're in the kitchen, Nate."

He was standing in the kitchen's wide entryway within seconds. He flashed Janine a smile then walked over to the kitchen island and picked up his daughter. He placed her on his hip. "How's daddy's little pumpkin doing today?"

He proceeded to touch his nose to hers, giving her a nose kiss. He smiled. "How you doing today, Pumpkin?"

"Daddy," she said, just as plain as day.

Nate's ears heard it, but he could barely believe it. His little girl had just called him daddy for the first time ever. When she said it again, Nate had to fight past his emotions. He was so overwhelmed that he hugged his daughter a little bit closer to his heart and just stood there holding her for almost two minutes, not uttering a word at all, just overabundantly grateful that his precious little angel had called him her dad.

As for Janine, she could barely believe her ears either. She'd worked with Lisa half the morning on coloring those crudely drawn pictures of Nate, but she hadn't expected to see results this quickly. Nate had been able to fight his tears. Janine wasn't as successful. She had to pull a paper towel off the roll on the countertop and dab at her eyes.

"Excuse me," she finally said, figuring that she needed to give Nate a little bit of time alone with his daughter. "I'm heading to the basement for a bit, you guys. Be back in a few."

As she made her way down those stairs, Janine whispered, "Thank you, Lord…thank you, Lord…thank you, Lord!"

*****

Two Heart's Unspoken Prayers

Ten Minutes Later:

When she heard footsteps on the stairs leading down to the basement, Janine looked up from the headboard she was designing on the laptop Nate had gifted her.

She'd been sitting in a chair at the drafting table. But when she saw Nate, she stood up.

Their eyes met and they locked gazes, just staring at each other for several seconds. Then Nate said, "Thank you." He did something next that Janine really hadn't been expecting: He wrapped his solid arms around her and gave her a heartfelt hug.

And Lisa hugged him right back because she understood why he was doing what he was doing. It wasn't anything romantic — far from it. It was simply him expressing his gratitude, his gratefulness.

"Thank you, Janine," he said again as he finally pulled back from their shared embrace.

"You're welcome." She smiled. "But it wasn't just me—"

"It was also God." He grinned, too.

"Yep, it was also God."

His eyes were sparkling with happiness and excitement when he said, "I know you're busy, but I feel so good about what just happened today that I wanna go out and celebrate. There's a little mom-and-pop ice cream parlor that Lisa loves to go to. Will you go there with us and get a celebratory ice cream cone? Like right now?"

Two Heart's Unspoken Prayers

His joy was way past contagious, so, Janine couldn't help but nod and say, "Yes. I'd be honored. We definitely should celebrate the blessing we received today."

*****

Nate and Janine both learned that "daddy" was obviously Lisa's new favorite word. Janine suspected that the little girl had been wanting to address her father for a long time; the precious angel just hadn't been able to figure out how to do it. Somehow, someway, Janine had given Lisa the key to accomplish what the little girl had thought was impossible. Now that they knew what worked — what communication procedure actually clicked in Lisa's head — Janine suspected that the sky was about to be the limit.

Sitting in the family room in an armchair across from the one Nate was sitting in, Janine set her plate of vegan soul food takeout — their dinner — on the side table and smiled. "I bet she's upstairs right now saying daddy in her sleep. What do you think, Nate? Should we go check on her?"

Proud, Nate chuckled. "It wouldn't surprise me if she is."

Janine sighed. "Yeah. Me either. Look at God, look at God, look at God."

Nate was grateful to the Lord for their blessing, but while Janine was saying "Look at

God", he was saying in his brain: *Look at you, beautiful.*

He was surprised that he was feeling that way, but he knew he had to accept it. He had to be honest with himself.

Earlier that day, when he'd given Janine a hug, he had felt the stirrings of attraction about fifteen seconds into their shared embrace. The hug had started out as something innocent and benign, before he knew it, a part of himself was wishing that he could hold onto Janine forever.

Initially, he'd chalked it up to being overwhelmed with the moment, he'd told himself that he was just overjoyed about hearing his daughter finally call him daddy, he'd thought that he was only being grateful that Janine had been instrumental in making his dream come true. All of those thoughts had been squashed when they went out to get ice cream cones earlier that day. The whole time they were on their outing, he'd kept feeling the same attraction. He knew then that it wasn't just misplaced emotions. He'd discovered that he was actually feeling something for the lovely sista sitting across from him. And he liked feeling that way.

"What? What's wrong, Nate?"

Nate tilted his head to the side as a thoughtful expression appeared on his face. *I gotta be careful about how I proceed with all of this.* That's what he thought to himself right before he asked, "You don't have a boyfriend or significant other who might wanna come fight me because I invited you to stay here, do you Janine?"

Thinking that she understood his concern, Janine shook her head and said, "Nope. I'm single. I don't have anybody who might come over here acting the fool and causing you and Lisa any grief. I understand where you're coming from because I've had a few friends who had over-the-top jealous boyfriends and such."

She's single! Yeah, boiiiiii! He smiled. "Oh, okay. And I'm single, too. So, you don't have to worry about anybody jumping out the bushes at you or trying to slash your tires."

She laughed. "Uh…it kinda sounds like you're talking from first-hand experience with that one. Should I be packing heat? Watching my back? Do you wanna elaborate, sir?"

He chuckled, too. "Nah…I just wanted to let you know, ease your mind in case you're concerned about those types of things. That's all."

Somehow, they ended up staying in that study talking about any and everything under the sun that evening. When Nate's alarm on his Smart Watch went off, alerting him that it was time for him to start getting ready for bed, he was disappointed. He was on the verge of ignoring the alarm and staying up for another hour or two, but his houseguest yawned, and he figured it would be best if he allowed her to go get some Z's.

When he finally went to bed that night, Nate had a smile on his face. He didn't know whether

Janine was his Mrs. Right — it was way too early for that — but he was happy to have her in his world.

A few months ago, he'd started entertaining the thought of having a special someone in his life again. That had surprised him because after Lisa's mother had walked out on him, he'd assumed that he'd just be single from then on out. That's how much his broken relationship had hurt him.

Lisa's mom — his ex-wife — had been a cheater and very deceptive. When she'd found out that Lisa had a disability, she had discarded the both of them like they were trash. That had killed Nate's trust in women because a part of himself had begun thinking that all women were like that.

But Janine is different. My heart is telling me that from the get-go. Thank you for sending her my way, Lord.

Nate didn't know for sure what the future would hold for him and Janine, but he was excited about the prospects.

As an image of Janine's smiling face appeared before his mind's eye, he thought to himself: *God might've just hooked a brotha up. He might have just sent me the woman that my heart has been secretly crying out and yearning for.*

CHAPTER NUMBER ELEVEN

Janine had been Lisa's unofficial nanny for a whole two weeks, and she already knew that once the gig was up, she was gonna be sad. Lisa didn't do a lot of talking, but she was adding words to her overall vocabulary bank every single day, and Janine thoroughly enjoyed the time that they spent together.

It honestly felt like she had known Lisa her whole life and that surprised Janine. And what surprised her even more is that she felt the same way about the little girl's father, too.

Nate had taken to going to work at Blackstone Manufacturing in the mornings but coming home an hour or two after the lunch hour so he could spend the rest of the day with Lisa. If something came up at his company, Donovan — Nate's vice president — or one of the other executives would call him and they would have a video conference. Janine liked the fact that he was such a dedicated dad.

Sitting in the family room that afternoon watching Nate interact with Lisa while she tweaked the design of one of the furniture pieces from the young adult line she was working on, Janine couldn't help but smile and think to herself: *He's the type of father that I would want for my kids someday*. And she really meant it. The care, concern, love, and patience that Nate showered on Lisa was a beautiful thing to witness.

When the doorbell began ringing, Janine set her laptop on the table and said, "You guys can keep playing. I'll go get the door."

Turns out, it was Nate's sister, Ayanna, visiting.

"Hey, hey, hey, everybody. I heard a miracle had happened and as soon as I got back into town, I had to come over and check it out for myself." She grinned at all three of them. "I hope y'all don't mind me stopping by unannounced."

Nate chuckled. "Don't you do that all the time, sis?"

Ayanna tilted her head to the side and placed a hand on her hip, pretending to be upset. Then she laughed, too. "Okay, okay…I can't deny that you're telling the truth. I was just trying to be a little bit more respectful, you know, since you got company nowadays, since Janine lives here, too." Her eyes met Janine's. "She might not wanna do a YouTube collab with me if she thinks I'm rude or disrespectful."

Nate laughed again. "She would never think that, Yana. I already explained to her that you're just my bratty little sister. You been that way since you were knee high to a grasshopper." He shrugged his shoulders. "I figured that you're probably not gonna change anytime soon, so…"

Two Heart's Unspoken Prayers

Ayanna made a pretend stink face. "Why you always gotta be mean to me like that, Nate? As soon as Mama and Daddy get back in town, I'm telling."

All three of them laughed at the silliness of it all, then Ayanna walked over and sat on the floor right beside her niece. She gave Lisa a hug then asked her how she was doing. By the time Ayanna was done talking to Lisa, she wanted to cry. That's just how happy she was. Her used to be almost totally nonverbal little niece was now forming complete sentences. True, they were short sentences — only three or four words — but the progress was just so astonishing. A miracle.

Ayanna looked over at Janine. "Wow, you really are something else, DesignSistah2000…" She smiled. "I mean Janine."

Janine grinned right back. "Like I been telling that brother of yours, it wasn't just me, it was God."

Ayanna nodded her head. "Amen to that."

Ayanna only spent another ten minutes or so there at Nate's house, but when she left, she was all smiles — and not just because she was happy that her niece was making such great progress. Nope, she was grinning because of the attraction that she had witnessed between her brother and his temporary nanny.

Driving the short distance home, she thought to herself: *I bet he hasn't even told her that he likes her. I'mma call his butt tonight and get the whole rundown. Big brother's gonna have to drop all that tea.*

*****

"Well, Nate, I'm actually surprised that you picked up your phone. I kinda suspected you were gonna be too busy spending some quality time with DesignSistah2000 just about now." She laughed. "I meant Janine, not DesignSistah2000. Lord knows I'mma have to get her YouTube handle out my head. But that's who I've been knowing her as for the past two years, so it's gonna take a minute for me to get it all straightened out in my brain."

"Uhm, what are you talking about, Ayanna?"

Ayanna sucked her teeth. "You can cut the act, big brother. It's me you're talking to. Like seriously. You have a thing for DesignSistah—" She playfully rolled her eyes in response to her mistake. "There I go again…tryna call her DesignSistah2000. But anyway, you know what I'm talking about. You're attracted to Janine."

Tell the truth and shame the devil. Nate saw no reason to try to hide the obvious from his sibling. "Okay. I'm attracted to her. I admit it."

"Well, have you told her yet?"

"Nope. I've been playing it cool. We've only known each other about four weeks. I don't wanna make any missteps. I wanna plan out how I'm gonna woo her, do it the right way. Plus, if we're meant to be, it'll happen. All things work for the good of them who love the Lord."

"Alright. I hear you, bro."

After Nate hung up the phone with his sister, he sat on his bed thinking about his attraction to Janine. The more time he spent with and around her, the more he realized that he was more than a little bit attracted to her, he was actually falling in love.

If anyone had told him that it was possible to fall in love with someone in three short weeks, he would've told them they were pulling his leg, he would've said they were lying. But that's exactly what was happening to him…what *had* happened to him.

He sighed. *I think it started that day four weeks ago when I first met her. I looked at the photo on her résumé, straight into her eyes and it was like I was seeing into her soul. It was something there that just drew me in. I think that's part of the reason why I changed my mind about firing her…why I ultimately decided to keep her on.*

"I'm falling in love," he whispered under his breath. "I'm truly falling in love."

*****

Over in Janine's Room:

"Hey, Janine. I know you don't go to bed till midnight, so I decided to give you a call real quick seeing that it's not even ten o'clock just yet. How you doing, boo?"

Janine sighed into her cell phone. "Hey, Vonda. I'm doing."

"Uh-oh... What's wrong, honey?"

Janine shook her head. She grimaced. "It's Nate. Girl, the more time I spend around that brotha, the more I think I'm starting to fall for him." Her frown deepened. "It's crazy, Vonda."

"What? You're catching feelings for your boss?"

Janine let out another sigh. "Yeah. I'm pretty much sure I am. I'm even having dreams about him, girl. And all this week, I've been sad and in a funk — even though I made sure I hid it from Nate and Lisa. I'mma hate it when my three weeks here are up next week and I have to move out. I'mma miss both of them something fierce."

"Maybe he feels the same way about you."

Janine shook her head. "Nah... I seriously doubt that. He don't feel the same way about me. He's been nice to me and everything, but he hasn't put out any signs that he's interested."

Because of what happened with Jermaine and how she'd vowed not to get attached again, Vonda knew that Lisa catching feelings for someone else was a big thing. Now it was her turn to let out a breath in a sad-sounding little sigh. "I'm sorry, honey."

"Yeah, me, too. I wasn't expecting to feel like this about him, Vonda. I tried to tell myself that it wasn't happening. But I can't keep denying the truth." She shook her head. "I'm probably gonna even look for me another job, cause I just don't think I can deal with being around him and not have a shot at being with him... Know what I mean?"

Vonda stayed on the phone with Janine a good half-hour, just being a kind ear and a support column. By the time they disconnected their call, Vonda told herself: *I'mma have to really pray for my girl. Lord, she ain't even got into a relationship with Nate, but I think not seeing him anymore is gonna be worse than the situation with that skunk, Jermaine. Fix it please, Jesus. Heal my bestie's breaking heart.*

*****

Back in Nate's Bedroom:

When Nate had walked past Janine's slightly ajar bedroom door fifteen minutes ago, he hadn't believed his ears when he heard her say into her phone that she thought she was falling for her boss. He really hadn't meant to eavesdrop — he'd simply been on his way downstairs to get a snack. Now that he'd heard her make that confession, he had a song in his soul.

He hadn't been sure that Janine was feeling for him what he'd been feeling for her — even though he kinda suspected it. Now that he knew the feelings were mutual, that changed how he was going to approach the entire situation.

115

With his snack forgotten about, he was lying on his bed with a big ol' grin on his face. *My beautiful angel is falling for me, too, Lord. She really is! Will you just look at that?!*

CHAPTER NUMBER TWELVE

The Following Morning:

"Hey, Ayanna, do you think you can keep Lisa for me this afternoon and evening?"

Ayanna smiled into her phone. "What, did you finally ask Janine out on a date? Is that why you want me to babysit?"

Happy that he was getting closer to claiming the sista who'd stolen his heart, Nate chuckled. "Something like that."

Ayanna's eyes widened because she hadn't been expecting to hear an answer of yes in response to her question. She was even left speechless for a few seconds. Recovered sufficiently, she finally smiled and said, "Sure can, bro. Do you wanna drop her off, or do you want me to pick her up?"

"Oh, I'll drop her off. Probably around three."

"Okay, you know I'm at home working on my YouTube channel full-time now. I'll be here waiting."

*****

After he left Blackstone Manufacturing a little before two that afternoon, Nate was all smiles as he made his way down the interstate heading home. When he walked through the front door of his home, gave his daughter a hug, and laid his eyes on Janine, he was grinning even harder. But his smile faltered when he saw the sad look in her lovely brown eyes.

He suspected that he knew the reason behind the look of melancholy that was on her face, but he asked anyway, "What's wrong, Janine? Are you okay?"

Of course, she immediately tried to make the look of sadness disappear. Her cover-up game was strong, but Nate could still tell that she was down. He wished like the dickens that he could just pull her into his arms and kiss the cobwebs away, but he had to take comfort in the fact that after tonight, she wouldn't have to be sad like that. *She'll know that our relationship doesn't have to end. She'll know that I care as much about her as she does about me — that we can begin building a future together.*

He gave the sista who'd captured his heart another tiny smile. "Janine, I know it's short notice, but I was hoping you could ride out to Morrisville with me this afternoon — it's only about a half-hour drive from here. I wanted to check out some hardwood selections at a timber liquidator out there…you know, make sure that it's the right stock for the young adult bedroom furniture collection that we've been working on."

Janine, forcing herself to appear normal, turned her lips up in what she hoped was a

118

convincing enough little smile. "Okay, Nate. You're the boss. Anything for my job."

She didn't really want to go on a thirty-minute road trip with him because she figured that sitting beside him in the car, pretending that everything was normal, would be torturous for her. But she couldn't come up with an excuse to opt out, and Nate was still her boss, after all. So that was it for that.

Nate and Janine had taken Lisa on various little road trips and jots around the city, but apart from the night that he'd driven her to his home after the fire, they hadn't been out together like they were doing now. Just him and her.

Since Janine suspected this would be their last ride together, she decided to try her best to enjoy it. To savor the moment. To file it in her memory bank for future reference.

She knew it was going to be a bittersweet undertaking, but at least she would leave with her memories of today. She was hoping that she could maybe look back on this day sometime in the future and smile.

Nate slipped his sunglasses on the bridge of his nose as they hit the interstate. Then he said to Janine, "Was it just me or did it seem like Pumpkin wanted to go with us?" He chuckled.

Lisa was definitely a subject that brought a smile to Janine's face, no matter how down she was feeling. So, she nodded her head, smiled, and said, "I kinda got that impression, too."

"I'm glad it wasn't just me thinking that. I sure am proud of all the progress she's made and I'm happy for everything you've done for her... for me, too."

"It was a pleasure, Nate. Lisa doesn't say much, but she's still such a joy to be around. I love talking to her and interacting with her. She makes me smile."

He definitely knew what she meant, so he nodded his head in agreement. "Every time I see you with my angel, I keep thinking about how you would make a great mom. How many kids do you want someday, Janine?" *Please say a lot of them because I definitely wanna give Lisa some sisters and brothers.*

His question made her sad again because she wasn't so sure that having kids was in her future. There was nobody for her to have kids with. Her ex had cheated — turned out to be a snake. And the man that she had just fallen for didn't even know she existed — not as a potential significant other anyway.

She sighed. "I love kids, Nate. I was hoping to someday have a large family. Four or five kiddos sounds about right to me."

"Yeah, those are my numbers, too. I know that I've told you before that besides Ayanna, I have three other siblings. It was good growing up in a family on the largish side. I wanna give Lisa three or four siblings."

Two Heart's Unspoken Prayers

Thinking about Nate being with another woman — a wife that wasn't her — made Lisa feel sick.

Seeing the look that suddenly showed up on her face, Nate frowned. He knew what was causing it, and he didn't want her to be in any more pain. Not of any kind.

He'd planned on them having a romantic dinner that evening, and while on that dinner date, he had planned on revealing to Janine how he felt about her. But all his heart wanted to do right now was end her suffering. They hadn't even gotten out of Durham when he took an exit off the interstate that would lead him to a quiet little park on the south side of town.

Janine was too upset to even notice the detour they were taking. It took her reading a banner that bore the park's name to glance over at Nate in confusion. By then, he was pulling into a parking spot under a beautiful grove of oak, elm, and dogwood trees.

She pulled her brows together. "Uh, what's going on, Nate?"

He let a breath out in a sigh as he turned in his seat to face her. He slowly reached over and took her hand into his. "I had a beautiful dinner planned this evening for just the two of us...you and me. This little trip outta town was supposed to be the diversion to give the caterers the chance to set up a private little oasis under the gazebo back at home." He smiled. "I had imagined us dining under the stars with beautiful smelling roses and lilies perfuming the air as I made my confession." With love in his heart, he gave her hand a tiny squeeze. "But I guess God had other plans."

She was beyond confused now. "What?"

"I've fallen in love with you, Janine. I was gonna tell you this evening and hope that you'd give me — give us — a chance. I know we haven't known each other for too long, but that's how I feel. I'm in love with you, girl, and after you move into your new apartment next week, I don't want the togetherness that we've built to end."

He finally frowned. "And this is not something I'm saying lightly. You see, I was married to Lisa's mom —Tasha. She cheated on me all the time, and after Lisa was born, when we found out she had a disability, Tasha dumped the both of us. She left me for another man who was making way more money than I was making at the time because my business hadn't taken off yet."

He shook his head just from thinking about it. "After that happened, I didn't think I'd ever fall for anyone again. I'd been hurt so badly that I was afraid of ever opening my heart, exposing myself to being burned like that all over." He reclaimed his smile. "But then you blew into my life and tore down every single barrier that I'd placed around my heart. I'm in love with you Janine. And all I want — all I need — is the opportunity to prove that to you."

Two Heart's Unspoken Prayers

He couldn't resist reaching out and gently cupping her soft cheek. "Please give me that chance, baby."

Her heart broke for how dirty his ex had done him, but it rejoiced at all the love she saw shining in his eyes. *He means it. He really, really means it! Lord, you searched my heart and answered my unspoken prayer.*

He slowly stroked her cheek. "Are you gonna give us a chance, beautiful?"

She nodded her head yes, and Nate couldn't help but close the distance between them and claim her lips to seal their agreement. His kiss, sweet yet sultry, offered a promise for tomorrow, hope for good days to come. When they finally pulled their lips apart and smiled at each other, Janine knew that this time things were going to be different. The Lord had smiled down on her and brought a true man of faith and conviction into her life.

CHAPTER NUMBER THIRTEEN

Watching Nate's SUV disappear as she looked out the window of her new apartment, Janine couldn't help but let out a wistful-sounding sigh. She'd been in her new digs exactly one day — well, eleven hours to be exact — and she missed living with Lisa and Nate something fierce already.

After they'd confessed their true feelings for each other a little over a week ago, they'd made it a point to actually begin the ritual of dating.

Nate had already told her that he really wanted to just drive her to the justice-of-the-peace and make her his. But he said he refused to do that because he didn't want to rob either one of them of a true courtship experience.

And what a courtship they were having. Nate had taken her on dates every day that week, and yes, they would be going on another one tomorrow.

Their very first official date had been the dinner in Nate's beautiful backyard that he'd secretly planned that day he was supposed to be taking her shopping for hardwood for the furniture collection she'd designed. They never made it to the lumber yard that day. They'd gone home and had their date instead.

Two Heart's Unspoken Prayers

The backyard had been so lovely. Nate had hired a small event crew to handle the entire ordeal. The gazebo had been decorated like it was part of a wedding. Wispy, feather-light tulle and real lilies had been draped from the ceiling of the backyard pavilion. And strings of tiny white lights had been hung, creating romantic ambience. There had been a two-person wait staff serving them a delicious dinner of Janine's favorite — roasted lamb chops with grilled asparagus tips. And yes, for dessert, Chantilly cake, another one of her favorites had been served.

Nate had definitely gone all out for their first date and Janine appreciated him for his efforts. So much so that she'd gotten the wait staff to snap pictures of them and the scene. She didn't need the pictures herself — she knew they'd always be in her mind. But she wanted them for the photo album that she intended to make, the one that would chronicle her and Nate's love story.

And what a story we're gonna have to tell. She smiled just from thinking about it.

She saw hopes, dreams, abundant happiness, and more kids in her and Nate's future. She knew every day wasn't going to be sunshine, but she was certain that her and her new beau could weather the storms.

When her cell phone began ringing, she still had a smile on her face.

"Hey, Janine. Now that you got yourself a new boo, it's hard for a sista to catch up with you. What's going on, girl?"

"Hey, Vonda. Well, I just spent my first day in my apartment, away from Nate and Lisa." She frowned. "And yeah, it sucks."

"Oh no, honey. Maybe you should just take him up on his offer to run down to the justice of the peace and get yourselves hitched up."

Janine shook her head. "Nah, you know I ain't about to do that. I don't need a really big wedding — something small in the backyard will be just fine — but I still wanna let my daddy walk me down that aisle."

"I heard that. Well, as for Lisa... how is she taking to you being gone? To you not living there with her and Nate 24/7?"

Janine rested her chin on her balled up fist as she looked out the window and contemplated that question for a few seconds. Images of Nate's little girl hugging her legs and acting like she didn't wanna let go a few minutes ago popped up in her head. She frowned. "Lisa's not enjoying it, but in time, I'm sure she'll start accepting it. Plus, Nate's mom will be back in town tomorrow. According to Nate, Lisa absolutely loves her grandma. Her grandfather, too. But since her grandma spends more time with her, she has a tighter bond to her. Know what I mean?"

"Yeah, I feel you. And his parents...when are you gonna meet them? Or better yet, are you excited about meeting them, or are you a little scared?"

Janine blew out a breath in a sigh. In all her relationships from the past, she'd never met the parents. Not even Jermaine's. This was about to be a first for her.

"You don't have to answer that, Janine. But something tells me that meeting his parents is gonna turn out just fine. He told you that you would love them, and that they would love you in return. His sister, Ayanna, also told you the same thing on a separate occasion. I highly doubt they would lie to you about something like that. They have no reason to."

"Yeah, I suspect you're right, Vonda.

*****

Two Days Later:

Despite the fact that she believed that everything would be okay between herself and Nate's parents, that didn't stop the butterflies from fluttering in Janine's stomach as she walked with Nate and Lisa to his parents' front door for a cookout they were having — it was a welcome home party in his mom and dad's honor.

Nate took Janine's hand in his and gave it a tiny squeeze of encouragement. "Like I said, sweetheart…they're gonna love you."

She managed to lift her lips in a tiny smile. "Right."

Two Heart's Unspoken Prayers

Two minutes into meeting Mr. and Mrs. Blackstone, Janine realized that she hadn't had a thing to worry about at all. Nate's parents accepted her and so did his other siblings who were at the cookout that day.

In the kitchen with Mrs. Blackstone and a few of the other female relatives in Nate's family, Janine was cutting and plating slices of cake while laughing at a joke Ayanna had just told.

Ayanna smirked at the girl she was sure was about to be her new sister-in-law. "See there, Janine…I told you that my mama would like you."

Mrs. Blackstone turned her lips upward. She nodded her head. "I sure do, Janine." She suddenly grimaced, then flipped the frown back into a smile. "I think my son made a good choice this time around. Maybe he'll hurry up and pop the question so we can pull off a late summer wedding. My youngest over there — Nate's sister, Imani — she's an event planner."

Imani laughed. "Mama's my biggest fan. But she's right, Janine. Just say the word and I'll squeeze a wedding in for you and my wonderful, fabulous big brother."

Janine grinned. "I'll keep that in mind."

*****

Over in Mr. Blackstone's Study:

"Son, when you first brought Tasha by the house, I wasn't feeling her, and even told you that she wasn't the one. It wasn't because I was trying to put bad karma on y'all's relationship, it's just that I could read her spirit, and I could tell that she wasn't gonna be any good for you. That girl had a dark side that she was trying to hide from e'erybody. But this new one that you got, she's different." He smiled. "I gotta admit I like her."

Nate couldn't help but grin in response. He was a grown man, but that didn't mean that he didn't want his father's approval.

The elder Mr. Blackstone continued speaking. "When you got with Tasha, I tried to warn you that you were just attracted to a big booty and a smile. When I recommended that y'all stop by the office for some pre-marital counseling, you had to almost drag her in there kicking and screaming." He shook his head. "But I'm sure this new one — Janine — she's gonna be running to my office ahead of you." He chuckled after he said that, and Nate did, too.

Nate grinned. "Yep. Janine told me the other day that before she gets married, she wants to attend a few counseling sessions with her soon-to-be spouse. I told her that you've been doing faith-based counseling for years — that you even have a master's in counseling & psychological science."

Mr. Blackstone's eyes lit up. "So, you asked her to marry you already? She said yes?"

Nate shook his head. "Not yet, pops. But I'm gonna make sure it happens."

Mr. Blackstone nodded in approval. "Well, you probably wanna make it happen sooner rather than later." He grinned again. "She's done wonders with my grandbaby. Lisa needs a mother like that girl in her life." He paused for a few seconds then added, "And she's done wonders for you, too, son. I haven't seen you this happy in a very long time."

Nate knew that was the truth. With God as his witness, he planned on making Janine the crown jewel in his life.

The elder Blackstone chuckled. "I can see what you're thinking, son. I look forward to seeing the two of you over at my office soon."

*****

The Following Day:

Church service had been phenomenal that morning. Janine had been attending services online the past several weeks. Today, she had finally shown up at Nate's church in person. The three of them had gone — Nate, Janine, and Lisa. However, Nate's mother had wanted to take Lisa home with her after services…which she had. So, that left Nate and Janine hitting the streets of the city as a couple.

They were walking hand in hand at the mall, basically just window shopping. when they came to the jewelry store on the third level. Nate looked over at her, grinned, and said, "You wanna go check out the ice they got, bae? More specifically, the rings? I can't ask you to marry me if I don't have a ring to put on your finger."

Janine couldn't say that she hadn't been expecting him to tell her something like that eventually — after all, they were both head over heels in love. All the same, she found herself getting excited.

"Can't hurt to look," she said.

They spent about a half-hour walking through the store, checking everything out. Janine felt like she'd looked at a thousand and one different rings, but it was probably only a couple hundred. Either way, she fell in love with a princess-cut blue diamond set in a narrow, intricately designed gold band.

"Ohhhh," she said, her eyes shining like the diamond she was staring at.

He smiled. "I take it this is the one?"

"Yeah. This is the one. No doubt about it."

"Is the diamond big enough for you, or do you need a larger one?"

She shook her head. "It's perfect just the way it is."

"It's a beauty, isn't it?" That's what the shop attendant asked them as he stood behind the glass storage case grinning at the attractive couple. "We have five sizes of this ring in the store…would you like to try it on?"

Janine was beyond excited, but the ring had a nine-thousand-dollar price tag. "Is it really nine grand?" she asked the shop attendant.

"Yes ma'am, it is."

Nate smiled. The price was within the budget he was looking at spending on Janine's engagement ring. "You wanna try it on, sweetheart. I'm kinda suspecting you do."

His encouragement is what convinced her. Once she had that ring on her finger, she didn't wanna take it off. The ring in the case was a little large on her finger, but the shopkeeper assured her they could order it in her size.

Five minutes later, they were walking out the jewelry store empty handed, but Janine was happy they'd shared the experience. She planned on talking to Nate about the price of engagement rings. She knew that financially, he was doing very well. But as far as she was concerned, nine thousand dollars for an engagement ring was a lot of money. The one that Jermaine, the snake, had given her had only cost twelve hundred.

As they stood in line at the smoothie stall, waiting to get their healthy fix, Nate asked her, "What's wrong, bae?"

"Nothing really." She shrugged her shoulders. She smiled. "Just trying to figure out the best way to ask you about the cost of that ring. I don't wanna insult you or—"

"Nine grand is fine. I had budgeted about fifteen grand for your engagement set. But I guess we need to have the talk about finances sooner rather than later."

Two Heart's Unspoken Prayers

The way he was talking made Janine really sense that them becoming husband and wife was right around the corner.

After checking out a few specialty shops, they finally made it to a men's clothing store and Janine talked Nate into giving her a mini fashion show. That had been a basket full of fun, and they'd both laughed lots and lots as he modeled various outfits.

As they finally walked back out to his SUV and Nate got the door for her, Janine couldn't help but think to herself: *Wow, Nate has a solid relationship with Christ, but he still knows how to lay back and have a good time. I always have so much fun with this man. I can definitely see him as being my best friend, my confidant, my lover, my everything outside of God* — she blushed at the lover part because they were both keeping to their vows of celibacy.

All the things she'd just thought about were things she'd always wanted to say she was able to see in her significant other. If she were completely honest with herself, she'd have to admit that Nate was the first man she'd dated who had them all.

Settling behind the wheel, Nate asked, "Are you alright over there, bae?"

Kind and sensitive to what I might be feeling...I gotta add those to my list. She smiled. "Yep, I'm just peachy."

CHAPTER NUMBER FOURTEEN

Just because Nate's mom was back in town, it didn't mean that Janine was interested in giving up quality with Lisa. She and Mrs. Blackstone — with Nate's support, of course —worked out a schedule where Janine would still get to work with Lisa four hours per day. But at the rate the precious little girl was advancing, they all knew it would only be a matter of time before she was ready for a more mainstream preschool.

Yes, the school would have to have some type of program for kids with special needs — specifically autism — but Lisa, with her increased grasp of vocabulary, would surely fit right in.

Janine had started back to going to work on-site for half-days. She felt blessed that she could work remotely from home, as well as from the building that housed Blackstone Manufacturing. Being in a relationship with the boss sure came with its perks.

Nate was on her mind that evening as she pulled out of the parking lot of her apartment complex and hit the interstate. But she wasn't headed to his place. She was headed to his sister's condo instead. Janine and Ayanna had been talking about doing a joint YouTube recording for weeks. They were finally about to make it happen, and the best part of everything: They were going live instead of prerecording their session.

Ayanna gave Janine a fond hug as soon as she stepped into her condo. "Welcome, welcome, Janine… You ready to get our session on and popping?"

Janine laughed as she held up the bag of crafting goodies she'd brought along. "Girl, we about to make some chic home décor on the cheap. I picked up all this stuff from Walmart and the dollar store for less than twenty bucks. By the time we're done using everything in this bag, it's gonna look like I spent at least a thousand dollars."

Ayanna beamed. "They don't call you DesignSista2000 for nothing, huh?"

Janine laughed again. "Nope, and right back atcha YannaTheBlingQueen. That's why your channel has over five hundred thousand subscribers."

Ayanna couldn't do nothing but smile at that because she knew it was true. "Come on girl, my studio's this way. Let's go make this thang happen."

They were half the way through the ninety-minute live session when Janine began noticing a flurry of live comments on the video saying: *Turn around and look!* And *Say yes girl, he cute!*

Janine pulled her eyebrows together in confusion, then she turned around. What she saw made her cover her mouth with both hands. Then tears of happiness tickled the corners of her eyes.

Two Heart's Unspoken Prayers

Her future was kneeling behind her on one knee, offering her the ring she'd fawned over two days ago in that jewelry story. "Marry me sweetheart. Will you please make me the happiest man on God's green Earth, Janine?"

In front of a live audience of over fifty-thousand viewers, Janine's lips were trembling as she told the man who'd stolen her heart, "Yes!"

*****

Across Town:

Tasha, Nate's ex-wife, sat herself down on her lumpy sofa and began eating her bowl of Ramen noodles. A few months ago, she would've been ordering expensive takeout, not caring how much it had cost. After all, her husband, Rex, had been a multimillionaire.

But he wasn't her husband anymore. The dead couldn't have spouses. He'd taken his own life via suicide.

Everything had been just rosy for Tasha when she'd been Mrs. Rex Henderson, wife of a talented investment broker. Just a few months ago, she'd been a New York City socialite — flitting around the city as one of Manhattan's wealthiest social butterflies. Unfortunately for her, her deceased husband hadn't told her that the millions he was making came from an illegal Ponzi scheme he'd cooked up.

Two Heart's Unspoken Prayers

Rex had stolen money from some of the wealthiest people in the world. And when the gig had been uncovered, he'd decided to off himself instead of face jail time — life in prison. And as for all his illegally gained Earthly possessions, they'd been confiscated by the authorities. The mansion he and Tasha had shared, the three vacation homes, the yachts, the foreign cars, the jewelry, the furs…yep, the US government had confiscated it all. Tasha had been lucky to leave New York with the clothes on her back and two grand in her pocket.

That had been two months ago, and all of that two grand was long gone.

She was now renting a room in a roach-infested motel and working as a waitress at a greasy spoon in the wall. She frowned because her dogs were barking as she sat there on that old sofa, the pain the result of her just completing a ten-hour shift.

She grimaced as her cell phone pinged, letting her know she'd received a text message. But she had to admit that she shouldn't have been frowning because at least her cell bill was paid up for a year — that's the type of cell phone plan her and Rex had been on.

The text message was from one of her old friends back in North Carolina. In Durham. She clicked on the link included and ended up at YouTube looking at a video. She narrowed her eyes as she leaned in and peered closer because one of the faces that she was looking at was very familiar.

Actually, two of them were, but she wasn't paying her ex-husband's sister, Ayanna, any attention. But what she was paying attention to though was her ex slipping a ring on some chick's finger.

"Wow. Nate's getting remarried. Good luck to him and homechick," she said out loud, dismissing them.

The video was still going, but she exited out of it as soon as her cell started ringing.

"Hey, Tasha. How you doing, old friend. Did you see the video I just sent you?"

Olivia had been Tasha's bestie back when she used to live in Durham. She hadn't talked to her in a minute though because when Tasha had found wealth with her now-deceased husband, she'd let everything in her old life go. Friends and family included.

"Yep, I saw a few seconds of it. That's good for Nate. He's getting remarried. Whoop-d-do."

"Oh, okay. I feel ya, boo. I see the angle you coming from. It's good to see that you done moved on. But that boy done did good for himself in the past couple of years."

The last Tasha had heard about Nate, he was struggling with his startup business, he was losing money and about to file bankruptcy. She'd told him a countless number of times that him going into business for himself had been a fool idea. He hadn't listened, so she'd had to step.

That prior knowledge of Nate being a loser prompted Tasha to ask her girl, "What're you talking about, Livy? What do you mean by he's done good for himself?"

Olivia sucked her teeth. "That business of his…he turned it around. He has close to a hundred employees. He bought a brand-new million-dollar house on the good side of town. He's rolling around in BMWs and Benzos…not the economy line, but the ones that start at over a hundred grand. Your ex is big-balling and shot-calling, boo."

"What?"

"Yeah. Look him up, Tasha. Blackstone Manufacturing. You'll see what I'm talking about."

"Thanks for letting me know about this, Olivia. It was good talking to you. We gonna have to do better at staying in touch. I'mma have to go now because I need to check this out."

"Alright, talk to you later, girl."

Using her phone's web browser, Tasha looked up Nate's company. Sure enough, her old bestie had been right.

"Well damn," she whispered under her breath. "I think I made a mistake in walking away from Nate." She scowled as she looked around her cheap motel room. "I could be living in the lap of luxury instead of in this ol' dump."

The mattress on the twin bed in her motel room smelled like urine, so she refused to sleep on it. Instead, she laid down on top of the thin bedsheet she'd thrown over the lumpy, old sofa. She was supposed to be going to sleep, but instead of that, she was thinking about Nate and what she could have right now if she still had his ring on her finger.

She grabbed her phone and dialed Olivia's number. As soon as Olivia answered, Tasha said, "Hey, girl. I'm trying to move back to Durham. Can you let me crash in your extra bedroom? I'll even sleep on your sofa if that's all you got to offer."

"My apartment only has two bedrooms and I'm renting out one of them. You can crash on the sofa for a few days though. If you tryna live here with me, I guess since you my girl, I'll only charge you a hundred bucks per month."

A hundred bucks? She gotta be kidding. But Tasha didn't say any of that out loud though. As far as she was concerned, she wouldn't be living with Olivia for long. She planned to get herself back into Nate's house. She was ready to reclaim her ex-husband.

CHAPTER NUMBER FIFTEEN

Given his single-father status, it was a rare occasion for Nate to actually be home alone. But here he sat on a Saturday morning, trying to figure out if he was gonna go outside and prune the shrubbery, or allow his regular lawn maintenance man to do it.

Nate loved gardening, but ever since he'd started really focusing on building his company a few years ago, he'd had to throw his gardening efforts to the wayside. He finally walked out his back door to his to garden shed and took out a large pair of gardening shears. He decided to do it himself this time around.

He was at the side of his house when he heard a car pulling into his driveway. He wasn't expecting company, so he looked up more than a little curious.

Tasha brought the twenty-two-year-old clunker that she'd pay a thousand dollars for a month ago to a stop in the spacious three-car driveway. As soon as she'd entered Nate's subdivision, she'd known for sure that her girl had been right about him making big bank nowadays.

The car she was now driving didn't fit in with the scenery. If a person had caught her out and about in town three months ago, that wouldn't have been the case. Her Jaguar would've looked like it fit in. It would've been comparable to — or even exceeded the value of — all the cars she saw parked in Nate's neighborhood…the Mercedes-Benz in his driveway included.

Tasha had quit her job in Baltimore and driven down to Olivia's place in Durham four days ago. Durham was Tasha's hometown, but on account of the circumstances that she'd left Durham under — cheating on Nate and discarding her child — she'd had no desire to go back home after her deceased husband, Rex, had committed suicide. She'd been too ashamed. She'd also known that people were gonna be snickering behind her back and pointing fingers in her face. She hadn't wanted to deal with any of that.

She looked around herself and smiled. The payoff from snagging Nate — getting him back into her clutches — would more than compensate for snickering and finger wagging, though. She was now prepared to face it all. She was up to the task.

She stepped out of her beat-up, ancient ride wearing a cute sundress that accented one of her best features — her ample cleavage. She hadn't gone over the top with her outfit though — even though she had wanted to. And why not? Well, according to her girl, Olivia, Nate was now claiming salvation and full of the Holy Spirit. So, she'd wanted to dress appropriately. She didn't want to give off harlot vibes. Tasha was smart enough to realize that she would never be able to get into Nate's good graces if she ran up to his front door looking skanky and scandalous, dressed in one of the form-fitting, all-out-there outfits that she really liked rocking.

She was ringing his doorbell when she jumped, startled by his deep voice as he said "Tasha" as he stood at the corner of his house holding a pair of gardening shears.

She placed a smile on her face. "Yes, Nate…it's me in the flesh. I would've called first, but I didn't think you'd take my call. I got your address from your cousin, Kathy, and I drove right over." She frowned. "I need to apologize to you, Nate. For everything that I did. For how I wronged you and our daughter." She shook her pretty head. "Apologizing like that isn't something that a person should do over the phone or in a text message. God put it on my heart to show up and tell you to your face. Now, I'll understand if you wanna be slow at accepting my apology, but God says in Luke 17:3 that if your brother or sister sins against you, rebuke them…but if they repent, forgive them." Wanting to sound even more convincing, she forced herself to sigh right before she added, "Even a sinner like myself wants forgiveness. I'm walking with Christ now — I've seen the evil of my ways — I'm a changed woman, Nate."

From the way Nate saw it, what the woman standing in front of him had done to him and his daughter was unforgivable. But being a man of faith, he knew that he had to rise above what his

143

flesh was telling him to do. His flesh was in his head shouting, "*Cuss her out and tell her to stay off your property*." But his spirit forced him to nod his head and say, "Alright, Tasha. I'm glad to hear that you've found Christ."

He wasn't ready to let the words, "I forgive you," slip from lips though. He had to work on doing that.

Good, it's working! That's what Tasha thought to herself as soon as she heard the last comment drop outta Nate's mouth. She placed a pleasant smile on her face. "Do you think we can go inside, sit down, and talk for a few minutes?" She forced herself to place a hopeful look on her face, and she knew the look had somewhat worked when he said, "Okay, I can give you a few minutes, but we have to stay out here and chat."

She nodded. She could work with that. "I was hoping that maybe I could see Lisa." She pointed towards the front door. "Is she inside?"

Nate thought it was a bit egregious that Tasha had rolled up on him like she had. Because it appeared that she had turned another leaf and was following Jesus, he'd been willing to give her some lead way and the benefit of the doubt. But her mentioning their daughter's name and wanting to speak to her pushed Nate over the top.

His eyes narrowed as they met hers. "Talk to Lisa? You wanna talk to the little girl that you turned your back on? You acted like Lisa didn't exist at all when we found out she had autism. You refused to look at her, to touch her. You went to court and relinquished your parental rights, even though I was begging you not to. Is that the Lisa you wanna talk to?"

The tone of his voice pissed her off. She'd come out there to sweet talk herself back into Nate's good graces, into his life. Unfortunately for her, because of the way that he was looking at her — like she was a despicable individual — Tasha dropped the ball. Her true nature came to the forefront.

"You're a real piece of work," she spat. "I didn't want that little brat anyways! You're the one who kept running around insisting that you wanted a child. You tried to ruin my life, Nate! I hate yo ass!"

She stomped back to her hooptie, threw the car into reverse, and angrily sped away from Nate's house like the devil himself was chasing her. She knew that she had messed up her plan to get Nate back as her husband. But that didn't matter to her right now because she had a new plan on her mind: Destroy Nate.

*****

Twenty Minutes Later:

When she heard her front door slamming, Olivia looked up from the sandwich she was eating while sitting on her sofa watching TV. She frowned. "What in the world is wrong with you, boo?"

Still hot, Tasha ground a single word from between her clenched teeth. "Nate."

"Uh-oh. I guess things didn't go as you planned when you made it to his house."

"Nah." She shook her head. "I can't stand his ass. He's a freaking hypocrite! He looking down his nose at me like I'm trash! I told him that I didn't wanna have no baby before he even knocked me up with that li'l retarded brat of his. He the one who kept insisting on me having her. Now he wanna blame me because I told him I didn't want her and signed over my parental rights. He's living over there in that big house on the hill acting like he saved, sanctified, and Holy! He ain't none of that! He was partying, drinking, and wilding out with the best of 'em when I met his ass!"

Olivia grimaced. "Wow, I'm sorry, Tasha. I guess that means you ain't gonna try to get back with him? Even for all that cheddar he got?"

Tasha shook her head. "Nah... I ain't going there. I ain't trying to get him back no more. But I'mma make Nate pay for how he just treated me."

Olivia, realizing just how vindictive her girl could be, felt sorry for Nate.

Scowling, Tasha asked, "What's his new chick's name, Olivia?"

"Janine. Why?"

She pulled out her cell phone and ignored Olivia's question. "She got a Facebook?"

Olivia rolled her eyes. "Girl, I don't know. I ain't friends with that heifer."

146

"Well, what's her last name then?"

Olivia shook her head. "Boo, like I just said, I don't know her like that. Just go to Nate's website…his company's website. In that YouTube video that she was doing with Ayanna the other day, Ayanna said that Janine and Nate met because she worked for him."

Tasha did exactly that. She found Janine listed as one of Nate's employees. She got her information from her employee profile page. Then she went and looked her up on Facebook.

"You find her yet, Tasha?"

Scrolling through Janine's social media profile, Tasha said, "Yep." Then she stopped scrolling when she noticed a very familiar name and face on Janine's friend list. "Whoa…will you just look at this? She's friends with Jermaine on FaceBook."

"Jermaine? Jermaine as in your cousin Jermaine?"

"Yeah."

"Ayanna said in that YouTube video that Janine used to live in Atlanta. And since Jermaine's been living in Atlanta for going on ten years, I guess it's not surprising that they know each other — even though Atlanta's a big city."

Tasha had cut off communications with Jermaine a couple of years ago when she'd left Durham and moved to New York — like she'd done with the rest of her family. But now she was intending on giving her older cousin a call and seeing if she could get more info on Janine.

"Did you hear me, Tasha?"

Tasha frowned. "What did you say, Olivia?"

Olivia shook her head and rolled her eyes again. "I had said why're you looking up information about Janine?"

Tasha looked over at Olivia like her girl was stupid. "Because she's Nate's fiancée. I'm looking for any and all avenues to bring him some pain. Plus, if he ain't gonna be with me, he ain't gonna be with nobody." She scoffed. "If I ain't happy, ain't nobody bouts to be happy."

"So, you're trying to find some dirt on her?"

"That and I'm scoping out the competition."

"Hold up... When you blew in here five minutes ago, you were acting like you'd given up on trying to get with Nate because you can't stand him. Now you're talking about scoping out the competition. You're sending out mixed messages, boo. Either you wanna get back with him or you don't."

Now that she was beginning to calm down a little bit, Tasha's rational-thinking mind was starting to assert itself, it was beginning to claim dominance in her head. "I'm doing my due diligence and getting all the info I might need early on instead of later in the game. I'mma figure out what needs to happen after I get my ducks in a row."

Two Heart's Unspoken Prayers

Tasha sucked her teeth. "Either way, I'm still gonna make happen what I need to make happen... Whether that means trying to get with Nate or destroy him. I'm not sure right now which one I wanna do. Okay? You feel me?"

Olivia felt her alright.

*****

An Hour Later:

Jermaine loved sleeping in on Saturdays, and this one was no exception as he rolled out of the bed that he'd shared the night before with his lover, Henry. He was headed to the bathroom when his cell phone started ringing on his nightstand causing him to backtrack and pick it up. The number on his caller ID was one that he hadn't seen in a long time. It was his cousin, Tasha. Tasha wasn't one of his favorite people, so he just let the call go to voicemail. He told himself that he would deal with her later.

That later didn't come for Jermaine until around dinnertime that day. That's when Tasha called him back two times and he figured he'd might as well go ahead and take care of talking to her.

"It's been a long time since I heard your voice, Tasha. What you need?"

Tasha sucked her teeth. "Why do I always have to need something when I'm calling you?"

"Because I haven't talked to you in almost two years, and you know that's the way our family rolls. Don't nobody call nobody unless they want something. Now, like I was saying, what do you need? And please don't let it be money because I've already told Aunt Rachel and all of y'all that I don't lend nobody my Benjamins."

Tasha felt like cursing her cousin out, but since she understood that a person couldn't draw bees with vinegar, she decided to use honey instead. She decided to be nice about it.

Placing a sweet smile on her face and an even sweeter tone in her voice, she said, "I wouldn't dream of asking you for money, Jermaine. When I was rolling in dough with Rex, I felt the exact same way that you do. So, I know where you coming from. But I *do* wanna ask you about someone that I think you know. I was on Facebook the other day and I ran across your page. I noticed that you're friends with a girl named Janine...Janine Grey. I wanted you to tell me what you know about her."

That was a surprise to him. One that caused Jermaine to scoff and say, "I haven't been on Facebook in ages, and I suspect that Janine hasn't either. Because if she had, she definitely would've deleted me as her Facebook friend."

Interesting. "Um, okay. I'll bite. Why is that? Why would she want to delete you?"

"She was my fiancée, but she caught me cheating."

Two Heart's Unspoken Prayers

"What? You were engaged to that heifer, and you cheated on her with another woman?"

Janine and Vonda had told all their friends about what he'd done, so Jermaine knew his sins were already out there. So, he figured he'd might as well just tell his cousin the truth. "She caught me with a man, and yes, it devastated her because she didn't know I swung both ways...that I was on the downlow."

Tasha was sure Jermaine probably thought that what he'd said had shocked her. It hadn't. Jermaine was five years older than her, but back when he had lived there in Durham, Tasha had caught him having relations with one of her teenaged friends. Jermaine had been nineteen at the time and Tasha's male friend had been fourteen. Being the sneaky person she was, Tasha had secretly recorded them in the act. She still had the video in the cloud — but Jermaine didn't know any of that.

Being the type of person that Janine seemed to be, Tasha imagined that her seeing her fiancée in such a compromising position had probably devastated her.

She cleared her throat. "Wow, that's interesting."

"Right. But why you wanna know about her though?"

"Because she's engaged to my ex now. My first husband, Nate."

"Wow. Small world."

She nodded. "Yep. Small world." She paused for exactly two seconds then added, "Well, thanks for the info, cousin. It was good talking to you, but I got an errand I gotta run." Yep, that was a lie.

"Alright. Bye, Tasha."

As soon as she got off the phone with Jermaine, Tasha laid back on the sleeper sofa that she was renting from Olivia. She didn't know how she was going to use what Jermaine had just told her to her advantage, but she knew she was gonna think of something. When it came to stuff like that, she always did.

*****

Across Town at Nate's House:

Nate placed the last dish in the dishwasher and got the cleansing cycle going. He figured that it was only fair that he clean up after the delicious meal Janine had just prepared for them. He knew that the kitchen wasn't a woman's place, but he could barely wait to get Janine in his home full time so he could sample more of her fabulous cuisine.

He smiled and patted his usually flat tummy that was slightly protruding now that he'd stuffed it full of ribs, mac & cheese, fried cabbage, and cornbread.

He felt a pair of soft arms sneak around his middle and knew that his fiancée was standing behind him.

Two Heart's Unspoken Prayers

Janine stood on her tiptoes and whispered into Nate's ear, "Lisa is now taking a nap, and I figured that you were so stuffed that you could barely walk, so I decided I'd come in here and offer my assistance."

Nate grinned as he turned around in Janine's arms, then locked his hands behind her back like she was doing to him. "Seems like to me that you strategically waited until you heard the dishwasher going, sweetheart."

She laughed because she knew she was busted. "Next time, I'mma have to peek around the corner to check on your kitchen cleaning progress and offer to help at the last minute, right *before* you turn the dishwasher on."

He smiled again. He couldn't help but feel content as he and his future stood there embracing each other. Janine was the total package. She was kind, Godly, beautiful, caring. She was a savvy professional in the workplace, but he could tell that she also loved taking care of her man and home.

He wasn't officially her man yet — they hadn't tied the knot — but he could tell that's the type of sista she was.

He frowned as his run-in with Tasha that afternoon popped up in his head. *Janine is Tasha's polar opposite.*

Noticing the look on her fiancée's handsome face, Janine asked, "What's wrong, bae?"

He sighed. He hadn't told his baby about his ex's little visit. But he was ready to do so now.

He finally pulled back and broke their embrace. He took her hand into his. "Let's go to the family room and talk."

As they covered the short distance, she asked, "Is this something I need to be worried about?"

"No. It's just something that I need to tell you."

He settled down into one corner of his comfortable sofa and reached out a hand indicating that she should sit down beside him — which she did. She got comfortable with her back against his chest, and he got comfortable, too, by looping an arm around her waist.

"Comfy?" he asked, just to be sure.

She nodded. "Very."

"Good." He slowly turned his lips up in a smile. "Me, too."

They sat there not saying a word for several seconds, then Nate said, "Tasha paid me a visit today while I was outside pruning the azaleas."

They'd had the talk about their exes, so Janine knew all about Tasha. "Okay," she said. "I thought she lived outta town."

"Yeah, me, too. But she rolled into my driveway demanding to see Lisa."

"Okay. She signed away her parental rights, but she *is* Lisa's biological mom. Are you gonna let her see her?"

Nate sighed. "I don't know, sweetheart. I'mma have to feel her out...see where her head and heart is. We've made so much progress with Lisa with your help. I don't wanna go backwards with my daughter. Something's telling me that Tasha has the power to nullify all the progress God's allowed us to make."

She sat up straight on the sofa, then turned and faced him. She took both his hands into hers. "I don't have an answer to what you should do about this situation, bae. But I know how to pray. So, let's pray on it."

And they did.

CHAPTER NUMBER SIXTEEN

A Week Later:

Tasha was tired as she flopped down on the sleeper sofa that she was renting in her girl's living room. Since she couldn't live with Olivia for free, she'd been forced to get another waitressing job. Days like today were the ones she wished she hadn't dropped outta school in the tenth grade.

What I need is a rich husband like Rex. Everything was peachy keen in my life when he was paying all the bills.

She looked down at her body. At thirty-four, she thought she was still cute. But the men with the big bucks were chasing after women in their twenties. Plus, she'd had a botched Brazilian butt lift that had left her rear-end disfigured. She'd set up surgery to get it worked on, but then Rex had been arrested and all their assets and money had been seized. So, she'd ended up not having the funds to pay for the corrective procedure. Most days, she hated looking at herself in full length mirrors.

Despite her physical imperfections, as far as she was concerned, Nate was still low-hanging fruit. *He was married to me before, we even kinda liked each other in the beginning. Plus, I'm his baby-*

mama. We can go there again — we can be married. She smiled to herself. *Then I would have access to his Benjamins.*

Tasha looked up as she heard then saw Olivia entering the apartment through the front door.

Olivia grinned as soon as she laid eyes on her friend. "Hey, girl…you decide on what you gonna do about Nate?"

A sly little smile slowly materialized on Tasha's face. "Yep. I'm getting my husband back. All I have to do is get Little Miss Perfect out my way."

Olivia lifted a brow. "Um, okay. And how are you gonna make that happen?"

Tasha began knitting her fingers together like she was a villain from a comic book strip. She smirked. "Oh, I have my ways."

"What? You ain't gonna tell me what you gonna do? How you gonna get that accomplished?"

Still smirking, Tasha shook her head. Then she said, "Nope. Just sit back and watch how the show plays out. In the meantime, you're gonna have to excuse me. I have an email to write."

"Well, okay, Ms. Secretive. I'm heading to my room."

Ten minutes later, Tasha was pressing the send button on her cell phone, shooting an email Janine's way. Tasha figured that Janine would be reading the email the following morning, seeing that she'd looked her up on Blackstone Manufacturing's website and sent the email to her work address.

It had been 9:13pm when Tasha had sent the email that Sunday evening. She was surprised that exactly thirty-six minutes later at 9:49pm she'd already received a reply, and the reply read: *Hello Tasha. Yes, you've reached Nate's fiancée, Janine. I understand you'd like to meet me and speak to me in private about working things out so we can be a blended family. I'm open to meeting with you. Shoot me another email about a good date & time. Mornings are good for me, Mon-Fri.*

By the time they were done with emailing back and forth a couple of times, Tasha was beyond pleased with herself. She'd be meeting Janine at Starbucks in the mall that Wednesday morning at 10:35.

"I'm meeting Little Miss Perfect three days from now," she whispered under her breath. "That should give me plenty of time to get what I need done. I might not have a high school diploma, but I'm good at video editing. My subscription to my online editing account doesn't expire until next month. I'll just go the library and use one of their computers, then I'll be just fine."

She grabbed her cell phone because she had one more strand to weave to complete the web of deceit she was creating. She stood up and went outside and sat in her car to make her phone call. That's because she needed to give the conversation that she was about to have the utmost of privacy. She knew it would best that way.

*****

Minutes Later at Jermaine's House in Atlanta:

Jermaine absolutely hated it when family called his cell phone after 10pm. So, he was scowling when his cousin, Tasha, refused to stop dialing his number.

She'd called him four times in the last ten minutes, and he was more than ready to put her on block.

He grabbed his phone and texted her a warning: *If this isn't an emergency, I can't talk right now. I don't mind blocking family 4 being disrespectful.*

Tasha got hot under the collar from that little response. Angry, she texted him back with: *It's an emergency. Pick up!!!*

"What's the emergency, Tasha?" That's what Jermaine barked into his phone the second he finally answered it.

"Well, I need to break up Janine and my ex-husband because I wanna remarry him. And I'mma need your help for that."

He scoffed. "And that's what you called me for? It sounds like that's an emergency for you, but it ain't got nothing to do with me."

She shook her head. "Uh, yes it does, because I'm about to tell Little Miss Perfect that

Nate slept with you. I'm gonna tell her that that's the real reason me and Nate broke up. And you're gonna go along with the story if she contacts you and asks you if it's true. She's never gonna marry Nate if she thinks he's on the downlow…you know, just like she didn't marry you. And the fact that Nate slept with you, her ex-fiancée, that's gonna make it even more devastating for her. She's gonna walk away from Nate and never look back."

He outright laughed at Tasha this time…for a full thirty seconds straight. When he was done chuckling — at least somewhat — he said, "My mama always said you were a little cray-cray, now I really do believe her."

Keeping her cool, even though she really wanted to fly off the handle, Tasha replied, "That day when you were nineteen and you decided to sex my friend Mike's younger brother, I was hiding in the closet recording the whole thing on my phone. After all these years, I still have the video — I uploaded it into the cloud. That boy was fourteen back then…you were nineteen. So, if you don't wanna end up in the slammer for a very long time, I recommend that you take what I'm saying real serious. And while you're at it, you can CashApp me five grand for hush money."

That shut Jermaine's laughter down with a quickness. "Show me some proof," he demanded in a quiet, serious-sounding voice.

Now it was her turn to chuckle. "I already did. I froze one of the frames of the video and blurred out y'all faces. I sent it to you while you were telling me how your mama said I was cray-cray. Who cray-cray now, Jermaine?" She laughed.

The beads of sweat that had popped up on his forehead were proof of the fear that was overpowering Jermaine as he stared at the photo his cousin had sent him. "Send me your CashApp handle," he said, his voice tight and angry.

She smirked. "That's what I'm talking about."

*****

Across Town:

Ever since they'd gotten engaged, Janine and Nate had made a habit of talking to each other before they went to bed at night. This night was no different.

"Hey, sweetheart," Nate said as soon as Janine answered her cell phone. "I know it's later than our usual call, but I couldn't let the day end without telling you goodnight."

Janine turned her lips up in a smile. She felt so blessed to have a man like Nate in her life. A man who craved her company. A man who kept her needs and wants on his mind. A man she could tell really and truly loved her.

He said, "You gonna tell me you feel the same way, too, aren't you?" Then he chuckled because he knew for sure how his baby felt about him.

Janine sighed. "Of course, sweetheart...I love you, Nate. I was quiet just now because I was sitting here thinking about how blessed and fortunate I am to have you in my life."

"It goes both ways, Janine. Before I met you, I was lonely. But now I don't have to be lonely anymore. God sent me a perfectly beautiful angel. I love you with my everything, with all that is in me." He grinned. "And one of the best parts about it is that I'm sure Lisa loves you like that, too. I can't wait until we get married and you officially adopt her... Thanks for wanting to do that, babe."

Adopting Lisa wasn't an afterthought for Janine. It was her heart's desire. "I really wanna be her mom, Nate. She stole my heart a long time ago."

Nate smiled. "Yeah. I think God showed her that you were gonna be her mama. I think that's why she opened up to you like she did."

Talking about being Lisa's mom brought the email communication that she'd had with Tasha to the forefront of Janine's mind. It prompted her to say, "You're not gonna believe this, but Tasha emailed me tonight. She wants us to meet — me and her — so that we can talk about ways to maybe work together so Lisa can have two moms to give her a double dose of love."

"What?"

"Yeah, I'm meeting with Tasha in a couple of days at the Starbucks in the mall. We're gonna talk about Lisa. I know that Tasha did you dirty, but based on what she was telling me in her email, it seems like she's turned a new leaf, that she's given her life to the Lord. God will change a person, sweetheart."

God will change a person. Nate knew that part was true because God had certainly changed him. He hadn't always been a man after God's heart, he'd been a scoundrel.

He finally gave his head a little nod and said, "Ok, bae. Just let me know how the meeting turns out. Like I told you, my little run-in with her the other day turned out to be a doozy…even though she texted me yesterday and apologized."

"I'll be sure to give you a blow-by-blow of our conversation. You'll be the first to know what she tells me, and how it turns out."

That was it for Nate and Janine's conversation about Tasha. They moved on to discussing another topic that was important to both of them: setting a wedding date!

When they finally got off the phone about fifteen minutes later, they were both grinning ear-to-ear, and they both had love shining from their eyes. They'd decided they were tired of beating around the bush and wanted to be together sooner rather than later. So, they would be exchanging their vows in six weeks.

That had been the perfect move for Janine. Why? She had always imagined an intimate little summer wedding. Being that the first week of September was still summer — and Durham was typically still very warm during that time of the year — she would be getting her heart's desire. On top of that, Nate's beautiful large backyard would be the perfect venue.

As she finally went to sleep that night, she had visions of being a beautiful bride and thoughts of her, Nate, and Lisa being a family on her mind.

CHAPTER NUMBER SEVENTEEN

Janine had a tight-knit relationship with both her parents, so she was all-smiles when her father called her the following evening while she was getting ready to make supper.

"Hey daddy, what's going on down there in Atlanta with you and mama?"

Carlton Grey turned his lips upward then said, "Nothing much. Just calling to see how my baby girl's doing?"

Seeing that things were going so well in her life right now, that was a subject that Janine was more than excited to talk about. "Everything's great, daddy. Nate and I just set a wedding date last night. It's gonna be the first Saturday in September. I know it's only six weeks away, but you and mama need to go ahead and clear y'all calendar."

Mr. Grey nodded his head. He smiled and then he frowned. "Okay, sugarplum."

It was the tone of his voice. That's how Janine knew that something was wrong. She was tight with her father. Ever since she'd been a pre-teen, she'd been good at reading him like that. "What is it, daddy?" she finally asked.

Mr. Grey began stroking his chin between his thumb and index finger. "Well, I had a disturbing dream last night, baby. It was about you...well you and your new fiancée."

Hearing her father say that made goosebumps pop up on the back of Janine's neck. There was something unique about her father. Most of the times when he had a dream — one that he actually had the urge to talk about — it ended up coming out as being true...at least in some form or fashion. Janine's mother — a strong woman of faith — had long ago told her that her dad had what true people of faith called The Gift of Prophecy. Janine hadn't believed her mother years ago. But now that she, herself, was after God's own heart, she believed it. The Bible made numerous references to the righteous being able to have visions and prophesize.

Janine sighed. "Okay, daddy...what was your dream about?"

"Well, in my dream, you and Nate were happy together, and Nate was treating you like you were his everything. He was treating you real special, and in my dream, he even had a halo over his head. But then a dark gray storm cloud — with a woman I don't know sitting in the middle of it — rolled over y'all house. And there was a banner over her head. It said: *Liar, Deceiver*. And then that dark gray storm cloud busted wide open with rain. Not just any ol' rain though...it was thunder storming on you and Nate. And then the wind from the storm blew y'all apart. Nate was screaming at you saying: *You know who I am, don't let the storm keep us apart, don't let the liar win—*," Mr. Grey shook his head, "—but you couldn't hear him because of the thunder in the storm. Then I woke up sweating."

Janine's frown deepened. "And that was it, Daddy?"

He sighed. "Yep."

Janine shook her head. "Wow, that was some dream."

"I know, right? It gave me the trembles, and you already know that don't much scare your ol' man. But you're my daughter, so having a dream like that about you makes me feel a li'l bit uncomfortable."

"I understand, Daddy." She suddenly smiled. "But Nate and I have a wonderful relationship. I know that no relationships are a hundred percent perfect — you and mama taught me that — but you have nothing to worry about."

Janine and her father then talked about her upcoming nuptials. When she finally got off the phone with her dad a half hour later, Janine was all smiles. She couldn't wait for her daddy to walk her down the aisle. And she knew that he could barely wait either.

*****

Now that she had a wedding to plan in a matter of only weeks, her nuptials were on the forefront of Janine's mind. But she still hadn't forgot about her upcoming meet-up with Nate's ex, Tasha.

She walked out of Blackstone Manufacturing at ten o'clock and made her way to the Starbucks in the mall. Right before she could enter the building though, a homeless woman standing outside the entry doors smiled at her. Janine had been down on her luck in her life before, so most of the time, she didn't mind given a little something to the people on the streets that many others labeled vagabond.

Janine returned the woman's smile with a warm, genuine one of her own, ignoring the mild stench she could smell emanating from the woman's dingy clothing. Janine paired, "How're you doing today, ma'am?" with her smile.

"Oh, I'm doing okay. God is taking care of me. And how're you doing today, young lady?"

"I'm good." Janine turned her grin up a notch. "And like you, God is taking care of me, too." Janine suddenly had the strongest urge to be of assistance to the middle-aged woman standing in front of her. "Do you need anything? A meal maybe?"

The woman's eyes lit up. "I could use a smoothie…strawberry mango. They sell 'em in there in the mall on the second floor."

Janine winked an eye. "I'll be back with a large strawberry mango in a little bit."

Since Janine was early for her meeting with Tasha, she had plenty of time to get the smoothie and make it to Starbucks. She paid for the treat and went back outside to give it to its recipient.

"Here you go, ma'am. One large strawberry mango smoothie."

Grateful, the woman took the smoothie with a broad smile. And at the same time, she handed Janine a small piece of paper that she'd evidently scribbled something on. The woman winked an eye. "It's a Bible scripture that I really like. It's a blessing to be a blessing. You blessed me with this smoothie, now I'mma bless you with God's word."

Janine beamed. "It sure is a blessing to be a blessing. And thank you for the scripture."

Walking towards Starbucks, Janine read the scripture. It was Acts 2:17: *In the last days, God says, I will pour out my Spirit on all people. Your sons and daughters will prophesy, your young men will see visions, your old men will dream dreams.* And below the scripture the woman had written: *God sends you what you need, even before you know you need it. You just have to be willing to listen & accept it.*

"Hmmm," she said softly under her breath as she slipped the scripture into her purse for safekeeping.

A couple of minutes later, she ordered herself a frappuccino and found herself a table towards the back of the seating area. She was a little bit early, so she was a third of the way into her drink when she heard a female say her name.

Janine smiled up at the woman who looked a lot like Lisa. "Yes, I'm Janine. You must be Tasha."

"Yep, I'm Tasha." She reached out her palm for a handshake. She smiled. "It's nice to finally meet you, Janine. Thank you for coming." She claimed a seat at the little bistro table directly across from Janine.

Tasha loved Starbucks coffee. But at about five dollars a pop, it had been months since she'd indulged in the drink that she now considered to be a luxury — she hadn't had the extra money to.

Tasha frowned and said, "I accidentally left my credit card in the car, do you mind buying me a latte?"

Odd, but okay. Janine smiled as she reached into her purse and handed Tasha a ten-dollar bill. "Of course."

Five minutes later, both women were once again seated across from each other at the table Janine had snagged for them.

Tasha grinned. "Again, I'd like to say congratulations on your engagement. I really do pray that the Lord blesses your and Nate's union." She shook her head as she said, "I know things didn't work out between Nate and I, but that doesn't mean that I can't wish y'all happiness. That's what the Lord put on my heart to do."

"Thanks, Tasha."

"Yeah, you're welcome. And I already apologized to Nate for acting the fool when I dropped by his place the other day, but I'm a work

in progress, girl. God's still working on me." She
sighed. "I know you've probably heard the stories
about what a messed-up individual I am — how I
deserted Lisa and cheated on Nate. Yes, I signed
over custody of my beautiful little girl, and I now
know that was a mistake. But as for cheating on
Nate, that never would've happened if he hadn't
cheated on me first. I came home one day and found
him in bed with somebody else… He was getting
busy with another dude, girl. Nate was on the
downlow."

*Nate cheated on Tasha with a man? Nate's
on the downlow? It can't be…I must've heard her
wrong.* "What did you just say, Tasha?"

Tasha swiped her finger across her cell
phone and opened the video that she had
photoshopped the other night — the porn video clip
that she'd superimposed Nate and Jermaine's faces
on. She pushed her phone across the table towards
Janine. "Here you go, some people didn't believe
me when I tried to tell them how Nate really was.
But I got the proof right here. Like they say, the
proof's in the pudding."

As she watched the ten-second video clip,
Janine felt bile rising out her stomach and into her
throat. *No, it can't be. My Nate can't be on the
downlow. And on top of that, he had an
entanglement with that snake of an ex of mine,
Jermaine. No, Lord. No. No. No!*

Tasha had to fight really hard to keep herself
from smirking. She could tell from the look on

Janine's face that her little ploy was working. Feigning sincerity and concern, Tasha asked, "Are you okay over there, Janine?"

Janine swallowed the lump in her throat. She shook her head, stood up, and said, "I gotta go, Tasha."

Janine felt like she was having a panic attack, so she sat out there in her car, distraught, for almost a half-hour. It's not like she could've driven away anyways... Who can drive with tears blocking their vision?

Sitting in the mall enjoying herself, Tasha bought herself another coffee with the change that had come back from the ten that Janine had given her. Her ploy had worked. She was a happy camper that day. She was so happy that she pulled out her cell phone and texted Janine the video for good measure.

Tasha laughed. "Looking at that video again should put a little bit more salt in her open wound. I know her type. She's about to give Nate his walking papers right now. Then I can swoop in for the save." She couldn't stop herself from letting out another giddy chuckle.

CHAPTER NUMBER EIGHTEEN

Janine had called her phone three times that afternoon, so Vonda was starting to suspect something was wrong. But in the interest of keeping her job, Vonda told herself she'd have to wait until the end of her workday to call Janine back.

Vonda was on her fifteen-minute break when she began playing the video that her girl had just texted her. By the time she got to the end of the ten-second video, her mouth was gaping wide open.

She now understood why her bestie had been calling her all day.

She returned her girl's call with a quickness. As soon as Janine answered her phone, Vonda said, "Oh my God, I couldn't believe it when I saw it. I'm so sorry, honey."

Janine's voice was emotionless, empty when she said, "Yeah, me, too."

"What're you gonna do, Janine? I got some sick days I can take. I can drive up there to be with you."

It had been three hours since Tasha had dropped the bombshell on her, so Janine was all cried out. Hence, the emotionless tone in her voice when she said, "You don't have to do that, Vonda. I'm packing a bag. I'm driving back to Atlanta tonight. I'm going to my parents' place. I'mma crash in my old bedroom until I figure out what's next."

"Are you gonna confront him…confront Nate? Cause if you are, I want you to be real careful. Ain't no need for you going to jail over stabbing nobody. If you do that, that'll mean that he won. You feel me?"

Janine grimaced. "I don't wanna see his face, Vonda."

"I understand, sweetie." Then LaVonda suddenly had a thought. "That video…when did it happen? This week? Last week?"

Janine shook her head. "It was four or five years ago."

"So, Nate didn't cheat on you with Jermaine."

"I don't know. But that video I sent you is from when he was married to Lisa's mama. That's the reason they got a divorce." Her anger rose when she added, "He lied to me. Said they broke up because Tasha cheated. He conveniently left out what he did." She narrowed her eyes. "Nate is a liar, a deceiver. No telling what else he's willing to lie to me about." She let out a humorless little bark of laughter that was tinged with the pain she was feeling. "If I showed him the video, he'd probably lie and say it wasn't him…even with the evidence staring him straight in the face. Plus, after catching Jermaine sexing another man, I can't bring myself to be in a relationship with any man who was once on the downlow. So even if Nate don't swing both ways no more, I could never fully trust him. It's over for us, girl."

Janine felt tears begin to burn behind her eyelids once again. "God must hate me, boo. This makes two times in a row. And I was turnt all the way out over Nate…I was completely in love with him. I gave him my whole heart. He seemed so sensitive, so loyal, so God-fearing." She sniffled. "It just hurts so much, Vonda. It hurt so bad…"

Oh how Vonda wished she could give her bestie a hug right now. She knew for sure that Janine needed one.

Vonda let out a breath in a sigh. "I know the next few days and weeks aren't gonna be easy, Janine. But I'm gonna pray for you, sweetie. I'm gonna keep praying until God heals your heart. I'mma help you make it through this…just like I helped you make it past that lying snake, Jermaine. I'mma help you make it past this lying snake named Nate, too, honey."

By the time she disconnected her call with Vonda, Janine was glad she had such a good friend in her life.

She walked into her bedroom and pulled the zipper on her overnight bag. She was gonna miss Lisa just as much as she was gonna miss Nate. Thinking about Lisa made the tears start flowing again. She had to sit down on her bed and take several minutes to recover. When her cheeks were finally dry again, she grabbed her fully stuffed suitcase and began walking towards her front door.

As soon as she pulled the door open, Nate was standing on her stoop wearing a broad smile on his handsome face.

"Hey, sweetheart. I thought I'd come over and surprise you with a box of Godiva chocolates. I know they're your favorites." He chuckled. "I have sweeties for my sweetie. I know a brotha's 'bout to get some credit for that."

"You can take ya chocolates and shove 'em where the sun don't shine, Nate," she snarled as she snatched her engagement ring off her finger and shoved it into the breast pocket of the polo shirt he was wearing. "And you can put this piece of bling with it."

He pulled his brows together. "What?"

She began nodding her head. "I know all about you, and how you cheated on Tasha with a man. Oh yeah...I know all about it! Are you still on the downlow? Were you cheating on me, too, like you did Tasha?! Huh?!"

If the situation wasn't so serious, so dire, he would've told her how cute she looked when she was angry.

He frowned. "I never cheated on Tasha, Janine. And I've never laid down with any man...I don't roll like that. Never have and never will."

I can't believe he's just standing there calmly lying to me like that. She snatched her cell phone out her pocket and pulled up the video. She shoved her phone in his face. "Well, how do you explain this?! Huh?!"

176

Nate had no answer for what he was seeing. He couldn't believe it himself. He frowned as he shook his head. "That's not me, bae. There must be somebody out there who looks like me, cause that ain't me."

Realizing that he didn't intend on admitting the truth, Janine shook her head. "You're a real piece of work, Nate. And oh yeah, you can take your job and shove it where I told you to put the chocolates and the ring."

With that being said, she began to walk away. Nate couldn't let his future just leave him, so he grabbed her arm, causing her to stop walking. "That's not me in that video, sweetheart. I love you, Janine. I wouldn't lie to you like that. Don't leave me, baby. Please don't leave me."

Nate had never begged a woman for anything, and he'd always said that's something he wouldn't do. But he was begging that day, and he would beg a thousand times over if begging would keep the woman who'd stolen his heart in his life.

She narrowed her eyes as she looked at the hand he'd wrapped around her arm. Then she locked those same narrowed eyes with his. "What? On top of being a liar and deceiver, you're an abuser, too?"

He got the message. He would never hurt her...not even unintentionally. He let his hand drop and let her walk away from him. As her taillights disappeared in the distance, blurring with the cityscape, Nate felt like he'd lost his soul that night.

Two Heart's Unspoken Prayers

In Atlanta at Vonda's Place:

Vonda hit play on the video Janine had sent her for what had to have been the fiftieth time. She wasn't looking at the video because she was a freak, she was looking at it because something seemed off about it.

Her older brother, Jamal, was a computer geek. And he happened to be crashing at Vonda's apartment that night because his place was being fumigated.

Frowning, Vonda hollered, "Jamal, can you come out here for a minute? I got something I need to ask you."

"Give me a sec, sis," he shouted. "I'm about to make it to Level 20 on Urban Valley Termination…I'm about to win!"

Vonda shook her head because she knew that a second was gonna be several minutes. Her brother had been in there playing that video game for over an hour.

Jamal finally stepped out of Vonda's extra bedroom fifteen minutes later. "Okay, sis. What's up? What you need?"

Vonda picked up her cell phone and handed it to her sibling. "Now, I'mma warn you that this video ain't PG. But study it for a minute… Does something seem off?"

Two Heart's Unspoken Prayers

Jamal raised both brows when he began looking at the clip. "Whoa… you weren't lying about it not being PG. But other than that, somebody's got some real video editing skills. I wouldn't have been able to tell myself if I hadn't interned that summer at the CSI lab."

"What? The video's been edited? How?"

Jamal handed his sister back her phone. "Somebody switched out the faces. Both of them. Look at the edges where the neck meets the body. See how blurry both necks are? That's your first sign. Then look at the colors. The color of the bottom of both necks should blend in with the chest area. Whoever did this editing did an okay job. But the blending was nowhere close to perfect. And the lips on the first dude…if you look closely — somewhere around the seven second mark in the video — you can see the tiniest sliver of a second set of lips on his face."

"Are you sure, Jamal?"

Jamal tilted his neck to the side and gave his sister a look that clearly said: I can't believe you're asking me that question. He then smiled and said, "Hello… It's me you talking to, sis. I used to work in the field. Plus, I have a degree in forensic science. If you don't believe me, I can get my boy, Howie, to take a look at it and tell you the same thing. He still works at the CSI lab and video forensics is his specialty."

Vonda hadn't smiled since Janine had sent her that video earlier that day. She was finally grinning again. "Thank you, big bro. I knew all them brains you got in your head would come in handy someday."

Less than a minute later, Vonda was dialing Janine's cell phone. When the call went straight to voicemail, Vonda suspected that her girl had her phone on do-not-disturb mode. Janine had told her that she was leaving that night to drive back to Atlanta. Whenever Janine had to drive long distances, she often put her phone in do-not-disturb because she felt like it led to safer driving.

I'll call her tomorrow, Vonda thought to herself. *Or maybe drop by her parents' house to see her.* She smiled. *I can't wait to share this news with my girl. Thank you, Jesus! Hallelujah!!!*

*****

At Jermaine's House:

Standing on the balcony of his expensive, downtown Atlanta fifteenth-floor condo, Jermaine scowled at his cell phone like it had just done something to him. When someone kept rininging his doorbell, he lumbered over to the door, pulled it open and frowned.

"Wow, what's got a bee in your bonnet?" asked his co-worker and part-time lover, Henry, as he sauntered into Jermaine's apartment and sat down on his couch like he owned the place.

Angry, Jermaine closed his front door and crossed his arms over his broad chest as he glared at

Henry. He was glaring, but his hostile gaze wasn't for Henry, though. It was for his cousin, Tasha.

Henry wasn't an angel — he'd done some pretty messed up stuff, and he was still committing various white-collar illegal crimes like embezzling money from the law firm they were both working for. That's why Jermaine didn't hesitate to tell him, "My cousin, Tasha…she's the one who's got me pissed off. I told you I sent her 5K three days ago to keep her quiet about me sexing that underage boy…even though he was the one who approached me about getting dirty with him." His eyes burned with rage when he added, "How about I just got off the phone with her and she's asking for another 5K?" He shook his head. "I feel like she ain't gonna stop blackmailing me. I'm gonna be going along living my best life, and she's gonna pop up out the woodwork asking for more money."

When Jermaine pulled his brows together and the rage in his eyes was replaced with a gleam that Henry was very familiar with. The blond-haired, blue-eyed Henry turned his lips up in a sneaky little smirk. "So, what're you about to do about it? Plant some evidence on her and get her locked up like you did David when he was gunning for your job?"

Jermaine shook his head. "Nah…this is gonna take something a whole lot bigger than that. I'm about to snuff her candle out."

Henry was devious, but that comment made even his eyes grow big as twin saucers. "Snuff her out? You mean kill her?"

Jermaine trusted his friend...his off-and-on, long-time lover. So, he nodded his head and said, "Yeah."

Jermaine then proceeded to share with Henry his plans of getting a stolen car from a street-hustler who owed him a favor. After getting the vehicle, he planned on somehow luring Tasha to an abandoned house on the rough side of the city and then making her disappear forever.

After Jermaine finished sharing his plan, Henry frowned to himself. He, himself, had done a lot of devious things in his life, but he'd never murdered anybody and didn't plan on ever doing so. He didn't like the fact that he'd gotten himself tangled up with a killer.

CHAPTER NUMBER NINETEEN

Pulling into her parents' driveway at a little before midnight, Janine was tired. She had the weight of her breakup from Nate on her heart, coupled with the over five-hour drive she'd just completed nonstop.

Her parents weren't expecting her, so, she felt a little bad showing up on their front porch unannounced like she was about to do. But she was sure they would welcome her in.

Sitting in his living room catching the Late-Night Show while his beautiful wife was already in bed asleep, Carlton Grey frowned when he heard a car pulling into his driveway. One discreet peep out the corner of his window curtain revealed his daughter's car sitting out there in his driveway.

He walked over to the security alarm and deactivated it before Janine even had the chance to ring his doorbell.

The second he laid eyes on her pretty face, he knew something was wrong. Frowning, he said, "Come on in, baby girl, and tell Daddy what's the matter."

There was nothing like her father's love, so Janine — grown as she was — couldn't stop herself from throwing herself in daddy's arms and crying. Carlton simply embraced his daughter for a whole minute, not saying a word. He didn't know what was wrong, but his heart sure was breaking with hers.

When her tears had subsided somewhat, Carlton pulled back and asked, "What's wrong, baby girl?"

She shook her head. "Nate. I gave him his ring back. We're not getting married."

Mr. Grey sighed. "Come on in the kitchen. I'll get you a glass of warm milk and a cookie. Then we can talk about it."

Sitting there in her childhood home with cookies and milk — a treat her father had always given her when she was justifiably upset about something — Janine spilled the tea. She told her dad the whole story. When she was done speaking, Mr. Grey leaned back in his seat and his eyes met his only daughter's.

"Everything that you just told me sounds bad, sweetheart — I ain't even gonna deny that — but don't you think it's a little suspect that the video you're talking about came from his ex-wife. An ex-wife who hated his guts up until supposedly recently. I think you got what Jermaine did to you all up in your mind, Janine...clouding your vision."

She shook her head. "But the video, daddy."

"The video that came from an ex who despised him?" Mr. Grey sighed. "That dream that I was telling you about...I had it again last night, Janine. If you ask me, it was the Lord trying to send you a warning. I told you that in my dream, you and

Nate were happy. And then a storm cloud with a woman sitting in it rolled over y'all heads, and the words *Liar, Deceiver* were written on that girl's forehead. That storm separated you and Nate in my dream. Nate had a halo over his head, and he kept yelling at you, pleading with you not to let the deceiver win…but you couldn't hear him over the thunder."

Mr. Grey took his daughter's hand into his and gave it an affectionate little squeeze. "God often sends us what we need before we even know we need it — we just have to be willing to receive it. Something's telling me that he sent you that message well in advance, baby girl."

He stood up from his chair. "Now, I'm about to go to bed and give you some time to think about it. I don't know all the intricate details, but something don't feel right about what that girl did." He placed a loving kiss on Janine's forehead. "Night, princess. I'mma pray on it. You know where your old bedroom is. You're welcome to use it for as long as you need it. Love you."

"Love you, too, daddy."

Five minutes later, Janine was placing her overnight bag in the closet in her childhood bedroom. She reached inside her purse, fishing for her cell phone because she was ready to put it on its charger. As she placed her phone on the nightstand, she noticed that a little piece of white paper was stuck to it. Turns out, it was the note she'd gotten from the homeless woman yesterday.

Janine pulled the note off her phone and began reading it again: *Acts 2:17: In the last days, God says, I will pour out my Spirit on all people. Your sons and daughters will prophesy, your young men will see visions, your old men will dream dreams.*

Then she read the message that the woman had written below the scripture: *God sends you what you need, even before you know you need it. You just have to be willing to listen & accept it.*

Word for word, that last part of the note was almost exactly what her own father had just been telling her. And she knew that the scripture from the book of Acts was in reference to her own daddy's dream.

"You're trying to send me a message, aren't you, Lord?" She grimaced after she said that. "But video doesn't lie… I saw him with Jermaine with my own two eyes!"

Janine flopped down on the bed. She was so confused. Part of herself was telling her that God was trying to show her that Nate was innocent — that Tasha represented the liar, the deceiver in her father's dream. But the other part of herself… Well, it was believing the video, and her eyes were telling her that the video was undisputable evidence.

Not knowing what to believe, she just laid down on that bed, and since she was tired after the very trying day she'd had, she fell asleep.

CHAPTER NUMBER TWENTY

Tasha hated her new waitressing job in Durham even more than she hated the one she'd left in Baltimore a few weeks ago. At least at her old gig, she hadn't had to be at work until well after the sun was up. But here she was, walking out of Olivia's apartment at three-thirty in the morning because she had to be at her despised greasy-spoon-in-the-wall by four.

The fact that she knew she'd broken up Nate and Janine was the only thing that had a smile on her face as she hit the highway and began making her way towards the other side of the city.

The road was pretty empty — not an unusual thing for that time of the morning. She grimaced when the lone car behind her sped up and closed the distance between them, getting uncomfortably close to her bumper.

I should just slam on my brakes and then I'll have a fat insurance check in my pocket. But from the beat-up state of the clunker behind her, she figured there was a good chance that the person driving probably didn't have insurance…she certainly knew that she didn't. She hadn't been able to afford it.

"I don't need to get caught up in a car accident," she whispered under her breath. Then she let out a sigh of relief when the driver slowed down and moved to the other lane.

Her relief was short lived though, because the driver got right beside her and then started moving closer and closer like they were trying to sideswipe her and run her off the road.

The faster she would drive, the faster they would drive. When she tried to slow down, they did too.

"What the hell?!" That was the last thing Tasha said because the next sideswipe resulted in her driving off the dark pavement, losing control and tumbling down a ravine.

Pleased with himself, Jermaine chuckled. He hadn't thought it would be this easy, but since he was generally good at whatever he put his mind to, he wasn't surprised. Not one little bit. And the best part of it all, there had been no witnesses on that lonely stretch of highway at that early hour of the morning. The two of them had been driving close to 100mph, so he knew her injuries had been catastrophic — he didn't even need to try to venture down that ravine and take a look to know that. As an attorney, he'd successfully won enough personal injury cases to know what types of accidents resulted in the most fatalities. He was sure that his trifling cousin was a goner, and he was happy about that.

Bet her ass ain't gonna try to blackmail nobody else. Burn in hell, Tasha.

Two Heart's Unspoken Prayers

If he hadn't been so caught up in the victory he'd scored, perhaps he would've noticed what was going on behind him — the tractor-trailer that was barreling towards him because its overworked driver had fallen to sleep. When Jermaine finally happened to glance in the rear-view mirror of the stolen vehicle he was driving, it was way too late. That tractor trailer mowed over Jermaine's car, crushing it like a used soda can, all while he was in it. Jermaine's punishment for his crime was swift, his judgement final. That dark, winding highway claimed two souls that early Thursday morning.

*****

Three Hours Later:

"Baby girl, you got company! Vonda just pulled into the driveway!"

It had been a long time since Janine had heard her mother holler at her from downstairs using those exact words. She had to admit that it made her feel a little nostalgic. But the pain in her heart from Nate's deception overrode the warm memories of years past.

"Could you tell her to come up to my room, please, mama. I'mma run into the bathroom real quick."

Five minutes later, Janine was walking into her bedroom and catching a glimpse of her bestie sitting on the edge of her old full-sized bed.

189

Vonda grinned as soon as she saw her girl. "It's been a long time since I been up here in this room."

Janine wished that she could return her bestie's smile with one of her own. She couldn't.

Vonda wrapped both arms around Janine in a hug. "You already miss him so much, don't you, boo?"

Janine sniffled. "Yeah, girl. They say some loves you never get over losing. I think Nate is mine."

Vonda pulled back from their embrace smiling, and Janine just couldn't understand what she could possibly be smiling at, smiling about.

Vonda took both Janine's hands into hers. "What if you didn't have to give Nate up, Janine?"

Janine scowled. "He's a liar, a deceiver, Vonda."

"No, he's not. The video was a fake. Jamal confirmed it for me. And you know he used to work for CSI in their technology fraud division, so, we can trust him. According to Jamal, somebody with some serious skills lifted Jermaine and Nate's faces and placed them on those bodies in that bed." She shook her head. "I didn't even know such a thing could be done until Jamal told me about it and pointed it out on that video you sent me. Either Tasha has some above average editing skills, or she paid somebody to do it for her. Either way—"

"What?! Nate's innocent?!"

Vonda laughed. "Yeah, girl. He is."

Janine started crying again. But this time they were tears of happiness. Grinning like crazy, she said, "Sorry to put you out, bestie. Thanks for dropping by and telling me everything. But I gotta get dressed." She was already moving towards her open suitcase. "I gotta drive back to Durham."

Retracing her steps to the bedroom door, Vonda laughed. "That's right, go get yo man, boo."

*****

Six Hours Later:

As soon as she made it to the Bull City, Janine headed straight to Blackstone Manufacturing. It was going on one o'clock — an hour past noon — so she figured Nate would be in his office. She pulled into the parking spot that was specifically reserved for her and made her way up to the executive floor, smiling and waving at her fellow employees along the way.

Denise, the attendant at the receptionist desk, grinned at Janine as soon as she saw her face. "Hey, Janine, congratulations on that young adult line. I hear that the big box furniture stores are loving it."

Janine smiled right back. "Thank you, Denise. I sure did put my all into it. It's good to know that it was well received." Changing the subject she asked, "Is Nate in his office?"

"Nope. He left an hour ago. Said not to forward his calls. Said he was heading to his quiet place." She shrugged her shoulders. "Only God knows where his quiet place is because I sure don't."

But Janine did. Two weeks ago, he'd taken her to a quiet little lake in one of the city's lesser used public parks. He'd told her that he loved to go out there when he simply needed to think.

Janine flashed the receptionist a smile. "Alright, Denise. Thanks."

Fifteen minutes later, Janine was pulling into a parking spot at the park, right beside Nate's SUV. The lake was a two-minute walk away, and she quickly covered the distance. The man who'd stolen her heart was sitting alone on the pier in one of the wooden deck chairs, and Janine could see his Bible beside him.

Her footfalls were quiet on the chipped tree bark path, so he didn't hear her as she approached. He couldn't see her either because she was walking up on him from behind.

"I'm sorry, Bae," she said, suddenly fearful that he wouldn't accept her apology.

Nate didn't turn around. He didn't say a word. That caused Janine's apprehension to go up a couple of notches.

She swallowed the ball of nerves that was threatening to clog her throat and prevent her from talking. "I'm sorry, Nate. I shouldn't have run out on you like I did. I should've believed you. You gave me no reason to doubt you. Vonda's brother is a forensic scientist. He told her that the video was a fake…that Tasha video shopped it — or got somebody else to do it for her. Please say you'll forgive me, sweetheart. Please say you still wanna marry me, Nate. I love you. I don't wanna live without you. I love Lisa, too. I—"

The force of Nate's lips crushing hers stopped her spiel. He drank of her nectar like a man thirsty for life-giving water. And Janine kissed him right back, needing him as much as he needed her.

Finally dragging his lips away from Janine's because he could no longer do without air, Nate smiled. "I love you, too, babe. And just for the record, I forgive you. But I think I'mma need you to bake me one of your pineapple upside-down cakes as an I'm-sorry gift. And I want some chili, too. And some of that homemade cornbread like that pan that you made a couple of weeks ago."

Janine laughed because she would gladly fix her man a mountain of food as a token of apology. She was just happy they were back together. She was ecstatic that Nate still wanted her, that she was going to be his wife.

As they walked hand-in-hand back to their cars a half hour later, Janine said a silent thank you to her Lord and Savior. She knew that it had been his mercy that had brought her and her soulmate together, and that God had reached down from Heaven and answered both of their hearts' unspoken prayers.

EPILOGUE

Standing on her beautiful patio, under the twinkling summer stars, Janine could barely believe that it had been a whole year since she and Nate had exchanged their wedding vows. The venue — the backyard of the home they now shared — had been beautifully decorated by Nate's sister, Imani. Vonda had been Janine's matron-of-honor and of course, Lisa had been their flower girl. Like Janine had always dreamed of happening, her father had walked her down the aisle.

Despite having autism, Lisa was now flourishing in a great school that had a great kindergarten program for kids with special needs. She now had over four hundred words in her vocabulary that she used regularly. And yes, her parents knew that for sure because they were keeping count.

Before they'd gotten married, Janine had told Nate that she wanted to adopt Lisa. The adoption had officially gone through six months ago and Lisa was more than happy to call Janine mommy — it was now one of the five-year-old's favorite words.

Despite the fact that Tasha had signed away her parental rights, both Nate and Janine had been a little fearful that his ex would still try to find a way to stop Janine from adopting Lisa. That hadn't happened though.

Nate walked up to his beautiful wife from behind and placed his arms around her midsection in a loving embrace, flattening his palms on her round, pregnant belly.

"You okay, sweetheart?" he asked, concerned.

She sighed. "Yeah. I was just thinking about Tasha. Even though she was a real piece of work, she was still Lisa's mom, so it's sad that she died in that car accident. Do you think we should tell our pumpkin about Tasha someday...but just mention some of the good things that you remember about her?"

Nate placed a gentle kiss on the nape of his wife's neck. He sighed. "That's one of the things that I love the most about you, Mrs. Blackstone. You still try to find light in dark, dim situations. I think if Lisa asks about Tasha someday, that we can mention some good things about her then. I suppose that when she gets a lot older — like middle to upper teens — we can tell her the full truth. At the rate our baby girl's now advancing, I suspect she's gonna be able to live a prosperous, independent life...even with her autism."

Janine smiled at that. "Yeah, I haven't told you yet, but a week ago, my daddy had a vision that pretty much says the same. In his dream, he saw Lisa with her own apartment. She was even driving a car. And we know from experience how my daddy's dreams are so…"

Nate grinned, too, at that point. He was excited for the future. The God that he served was a wonderful one, a marvelous one…He was a God who answered hearts' unspoken prayers. As Nate and his beloved embraced on that patio that warm, summer evening, Nate was grateful for that, and he knew that would be the case, forever more, yes, forever.

FIRSTMAN PUBLICATIONS

Thank you for reading this book. On the following pages, we've provided previews of other great books by this author — stories that we feel you will thoroughly enjoy. Also, feel free to visit our website at WWW.FIRSTMANBOOKS.COM to:

*Register for FREE offers

*Sign up for our mailing list

*Check out additional great books by other Firstman Publications featured authors

*Order a FREE catalog

OTHER BOOKS BY NIKKI SMITH

By Grace I Fell for You

The Consequence of Faith

Mercy Through the Storm

The Doctor's Faith

Forgiven by Grace

The Best is yet to Come

A Blessed Destiny

Two Heart's Unspoken Prayers

Firstman Publications, P.O. Box 14302, Greensboro NC 27415

TOLL FREE: 1-800-729-4849   www.firstmanbooks.com   Email: fmp@firstmanbooks.com

DATE: _____

BILL TO

NAME _____ COMPANY _____
ADDRESS _____
CITY _____ ST ____ ZIP _____
Phone( ) _____ Fax( ) _____ E-Mail _____

SHIP TO

NAME _____ COMPANY _____
ADDRESS _____
CITY _____ ST ____ ZIP _____
Phone( ) _____ Fax( ) _____ E-Mail _____

Item Code	Book Title	How Many	Price Each	Total Price

TOTAL AMOUNT

SHIPPING: $3 for one book. $1 each additional book.

SALES TAX: N.C. Add 7%

GRAND TOTAL

☐ Money Order enclosed payable to Firstman Publications   -OR-

Credit Card Number _____
Name on Card _____
Expiration Date _____ CVV Code _____
Signature _____

You may photocopy this page and use the copies as your fax or mail order forms.

199

Thank you for taking the time to read this book. I pray that you thoroughly enjoyed it!

With Much Love,

Nikki

Made in the USA
Las Vegas, NV
31 March 2022